FIGURES AT THE THRESHOLD

A Novel in Fifteen Religious Conversions

by Jorge Pinto Mazal

JORGE
PINTO
BOOKS

Figures at the Threshold

A Novel in Fifteen Religious Conversions

Copyright Page

Figures at the Threshold *A Novel in Fifteen Religious Conversions*

By Jorge Pinto Mazal

Published by Jorge Pinto Books Inc. 3101 New Mexico Avenue NW Washington, DC 20016 United States of America

ISBN: 979-8-9941995-4-1

First Edition

Printed in the United States of America

This is a work of fiction. The contemporary narrator, Daniel Ferrara, and the framing material in his voice are imagined. The historical figures of the fifteen chapters — Spinoza, Pascal, Heine, Mendelssohn, Newman, Huysmans, Claudel, Rosenzweig, Conze, Schoenberg, Stein, Weil and Benjamin, Greene and Waugh, Messiaen, and Pärt — are real persons; the documented dates, places, and events of their lives are presented as the historical record reports them, with disciplined imaginative reconstruction in the white spaces the archives leave open.

This book was written in active collaboration with Claude, an artificial intelligence developed by Anthropic. The conception, judgment, voice, and editorial direction throughout are the author's. A fuller account of the collaboration appears in the *Note on the Collaboration* at the end of this volume.

Figures at the Threshold

Prologue

The apartment is on the thirty-eighth floor. From the north window I can watch the morning light come down the new towers — 432 Park, Central Park Tower, 111 West 57th — and reach the brick of the older buildings on the side streets only afterward, by reflection. The building was the prime address in this part of Manhattan in 2000. I moved in 2008. The most photographed of the early residents have either died or moved up to the Carnegie Hill towers. I have not. I find I prefer a building whose moment has passed.

The lobby on Lexington, with its share of the Bloomberg offices, has the manner of someone still trying. The interior courtyard, which is the entrance I use, has the manner of someone no longer bothering. The restaurant at the front of the plaza was Le Cirque for ten years; whether it still is, in some renamed configuration, I am not always sure. I do not eat there. I greet the doormen each morning. They are not the same doormen who were here when I arrived.

I am seventy-eight. My wife, Marie-Claire, died three years ago this October. We had been married for forty-four years. She is not, in my private register, a memory; she is more an absence with edges. The edges are the chairs she sat in, the second shelf I have not been able to make myself reorganize, the small Nespresso cup she used for her morning coffee, which I have continued to use because the thought of putting it back in the cabinet is more than I can entertain. My daughter Isabel — public-health researcher, Boston, forty-two, two children — visits every six weeks. I take the Acela to her in between.

This is not a book about my wife. I want to say that clearly at the beginning, because it is the temptation that opens up most easily under one's hand when one is seventy-eight and has lost a person and has decided to write something. I do not intend to write about Marie-Claire. I intend to write about other people — a dozen or so, dead between three hundred and seventy years and forty years ago, scattered across Europe and America — and I intend to write about them by the rules of the lawyer that I have been most of my life, because I want to know something specific about them. Marie-Claire is the floor under the inquiry, not its subject.

What I want to know is what happened to these people in the hour they crossed the threshold of a religion. Or refused to cross it. Or, having crossed it earlier, were forced to decide whether to remain. I do not want what the convert later said about the conversion in the memoir. The memoirs are written by a different person than the one who turned. I want the one who turned, before the memoir.

I am not a religious man. I should also say this clearly. I was not raised in any religion. Religion in my parents' household was absent in all forms. We were an agnostic family — my father agnostic, my mother agnostic — and the silence about religion in the house was not an avoidance, it was simply the air of the place. I attended a school in Mexico City founded by Spanish Republican refugees who had come to Mexico after the civil war. The school was liberal, secular, fiercely anti-clerical, the kind of school you could attend in Mexico in those years because the separation of church and state was a serious public commitment, not a polite formula. I learned Latin in the Spanish humanist sense, not in the catechetical one. I learned to take ideas without sectarian inflection. I have not stopped doing it.

My father's family had emigrated from a town in Puglia at the end of the nineteenth century, come through Veracruz, settled in Mexico City. Behind them was a line that had been Spanish Sephardic before it had become Italian Catholic — driven into Puglia after 1492, displaced again by the Kingdom of Naples expulsions of the sixteenth century, faded into the southern-Italian Catholic majority over the slow centuries that followed. By the time my grandparents reached Veracruz they were Catholic in the mild Italian way that did not survive the Atlantic. My mother's family were non-practicing Sephardic Jews on both sides, several generations from any active observance. She married my father in 1935, in Mexico City, in a civil ceremony. They had a son who died at four. I came after.

The brother was a mystery to me until I became aware of his existence in my late teens. My parents had decided not to speak of him — because I was either already born or about to be born, and they did not want me to grow up in an environment of sadness that they themselves were, I am certain, internally enduring. I learned about him from an aunt, in passing, the way one learns most family facts of consequence. I have never asked my mother or father directly. By the time I was old enough to have asked, the silence around the boy had been the household's settled shape for so long that to break it would have been a transgression of a different order than the silence itself.

I attended Yale on a scholarship I had not believed I would receive. Yale Law followed. I was admitted to the bar in New York in the mid-seventies, joined a small constitutional-specialty firm in Washington, and met Marie-Claire there. She was a paralegal in her last year before her own law school. She was twenty-five, from New Orleans, of Creole and French-Louisiana descent, Catholic by upbringing in the manner that city produces — French-inflected, the saints and the Mass woven into the same fabric as Mardi Gras and red beans on Mondays. We married eleven months after we met. The week after the wedding, with her in the front row of the courtroom in the Southern District, I took the oath of citizenship.

{

• • •

}

The trigger for the inquiry — the public trigger; the private one came later — was a podcast. David Runciman's *Past, Present, Future*. The host is a Cambridge political scientist. He had recently produced a series of episodes on what he called *political conversions*: socialism to fascism in the first; the renunciants of Communism in the 1930s and 40s in the second; the migration in mid-century America from Trotskyism to neoconservatism in the third. I listened on three consecutive evenings. On the morning of the fourth I sat at my desk with a cup of coffee, looking at the north window, and noticed that the political-conversion frame was not where my attention had gone.

What had stayed with me was the *form* of the conversion itself, irrespective of its content. The fact that a human mind can hold a position for ten or twenty or forty years and then renounce it and take up its opposite, not as a gesture but with the whole weight of the person committed to the new position the way it had been committed to the old. The mechanics of the turn. What Runciman's converts had in common with each other was the political topic of his series. What they had in common with all the other converts in human history — religious, intellectual, the converts who had crossed without arriving and the converts who had arrived without quite crossing — was a question I had not heard discussed in the podcast. It was the question that interested me.

I have been reading Benjamin Constant for forty years, mostly for his ardent defense of individual liberty against the state and for the *Acte Additionnel* of the Hundred Days — the constitution Constant drafted for Napoleon between Elba and Waterloo, in the spring of 1815. I read him less often for the religion. When I did, I read him as a historian of forms. I have his *De la religion considérée dans sa source, ses formes et ses développements* — five volumes, the 1824 edition my mother bought in a Mexico City bookshop in 1959 and which I inherited along with the rest of her library when she died in 2002 — on the third shelf of the case behind my desk. Constant takes the religious sentiment as a constant of human nature and the religious *forms* as the variable. Sitting at the desk that morning of the fourth day, I thought I had been reading him slightly wrong. The interesting site of the inquiry is not in the forms themselves but in the moment a person crosses from one form into another, or from no form into a form, or from a form into nothing. That is the moment in which the religious sentiment is most exposed. It is also the moment at which a person joins a new community while leaving another behind — a transition that carries, I believe, weights of consequence that political conversion in our own century, for all its drama, does not approach.

This is not yet a theory. It is an instinct of a place to look.

{

• • •

}

The private trigger came two days later. I was in the courtyard on a Tuesday morning, having coffee with Ingrid Brunner. Ingrid is a Swiss widow on the thirty-second floor; her husband Henrik, an engineer, died in 2019; she stayed. She is seventy-three. We have coffee in the courtyard twice a week when the weather permits.

She put down her cup and said: *Daniel, have you ever thought about converting yourself?*

I said: *To what?*

She said: *I know perfectly well that you are a natural agnostic, without doubts and without prejudice. I know that you do not like organized religion. I know that if you were anything you would be a Spinozist with no need for intermediaries. I am not asking you to give an account of yourself. I am asking whether you have considered that the questions you have are religious questions, and what you propose to do with them.*

I said: *I don't think I am going to convert. If I were ever called I could try to emulate Simone Weil.*

She did not laugh. She said: *That is not really a joke, Daniel. Weil was called and she did not become a Catholic, and the reason she gave was a serious reason, and her not converting was as much a religious act as any of the converts' converting. You should not pretend that your not-converting is a non-religious act.*

I sat with that for a minute. The courtyard was filling. A man came out of the door from Lexington with a Yorkshire terrier on a leash. Ingrid signaled the waiter for the check. She said, more gently: *You should consider what you are doing. If you are conducting a religious inquiry, that is a thing in itself. It is not a substitute for conversion and it is not an evasion of it. It is a different kind of seriousness. But it is a seriousness.*

I went up to the apartment, sat at the desk. The window faced north. I did not move for a long time.

{

• • •

}

I am, by habit and by training, suspicious of language that elevates ordinary processes into spiritual events. What happened at the desk was that I sat there for an hour and a half and at the end had decided to undertake a piece of work.

What I weighed was this. Ingrid was correct that I had religious questions. I had had them since at least the year my mother died, in 2002. There had been no religious ceremony — as there had been none for my father, and, if I remember rightly, none for my grandparents either. We arranged the cremation for the next day, took the urn to a forest outside the city with a small number of close friends, scattered the ashes there, and held a reception afterward at her house. In the days surrounding all of this I was being asked by Jewish acquaintances who had not known her religion why we had not sat *shiva;* and by Catholic acquaintances who had not known her religion either, whether there would be a Mass. I had answered both groups politely with explanations that did not quite explain. I had had the questions more sharply since Marie-Claire's diagnosis. She had returned to the Mass in the last two years — daily, at the small chapel at Weill Cornell during the treatments, and at her parish on weekends when she was at home. I had driven her. I had sat in the corridor outside while she was inside. I never went in with her. I had had the questions most sharply in the months since her death.

What I weighed against the questions was the lawyer's instinct that one does not pursue a question of consequence through one's own internal monologue. One pursues it through the record. The record, in this case, was a body of human cases — men and women, over the past four hundred years, who had moved across the threshold of a religion or had refused to move, under pressures that were variously political, professional, social, intellectual, and personal. I am not, myself, under any of these pressures. I do not face exclusion from a profession, expulsion from a state, the loss of a community, the demand from any quarter that I declare myself one thing or another. I do not need a new identity, and certainly not an identity grounded in faith. I am an individual who cherishes freedom. My situation is not theirs. My interest is not the interest of one who needs to choose; it is the interest of an amateur historian, prompted by Runciman, applied — as Runciman did not apply it — to the religious case, where the stakes for the figures themselves were greater than they were for the political converts of the last century.

I decided to write about them. Not academically. I am not a scholar; I do not have the languages I would need; the libraries are no longer what they were. I would write about them in the manner I had once envied without admitting that I envied it, the manner of the literary imagination. I would do the reading and I would build, around what the record showed, an interior life I would not pretend was theirs in fact but which I would construct with the rigor that the record permitted. In each case I would weigh the contributing forces — the historical context the figure was inside; any persecution they faced or feared; the professional interest or material need that bore on the decision; and where applicable, the true belief, the genuine spiritual conviction, of which Simone Weil is the unsurpassed example. I would attempt to enter, by the only door available to me, the hour in which they had turned. I would not pretend to know what they had felt. I would ask the question by means of trying to write it.

I made a list on the back of a copy of the building's annual proxy statement. The list contained, in the order it occurred to me: Spinoza, Pascal, Heine, Newman, Huysmans, Claudel, Rosenzweig, Schoenberg, Edith Stein, Weil, Greene, Waugh, Messiaen, Pärt. After Spinoza I added Felix Mendelssohn — not for his conversion but for the fact that he had grown up inside one. I noticed I had placed Spinoza first. Of course. He was the figure on my mother's side. He was the figure whose excommunication, in 1656, in the Portuguese synagogue in Amsterdam, had been the first time in modern history that a man had been thrown out of a religion for thinking and had walked away from religion without converting to another one. I would begin with him. Not because I am Sephardic — I am not, in any active sense, anything — but because Spinoza's refusal was the foundational instance of the kind of refusal the rest of the figures would, in their various ways, be answering or extending or resisting.

{

• • •

}

On the bookshelf to my right there is a photograph, in an Art Nouveau frame I have always loved — gilded brass with the long whiplash curves of 1905 or thereabouts, presumably acquired by an aunt to dignify what was already by then an old picture — of a man in a tallit, taken some time around 1880 from the look of the print. The man is one of my mother's great-uncles; she did not know which one. The photograph was given to her by an aunt who said, at the time, that she did not know either. The man's face is not legible; the print has darkened at the edges. The tallit is unmistakable. He is holding a book; one cannot tell what book.

I have lived with this photograph for thirty years. For most of those thirty years I did not look at it more than once or twice a year. Since Ingrid's question I have been looking at it every morning.

I visited the Esnoga in Amsterdam — the Portuguese synagogue, the building Spinoza was thrown out of, except that the building was a different building then, a converted warehouse on the Houtgracht; the present Esnoga was consecrated in 1675, two years before Spinoza died. I went in 2014, as a tourist, with Marie-Claire. The benches are dark wood; the brass chandeliers are heavy; the sand on the floor is the original Sephardic custom. Marie-Claire said: *It is colder than I expected.* I said: *Yes.* We did not stay long.

{

• • •

}

I begin, then, with Spinoza. The day of the *herem*. July 27, 1656. He was twenty-three. He was at that hour somewhere in Amsterdam — not in the synagogue; he had refused to attend; he had been told the ceremony was being prepared and had stayed away. The Portuguese community read the *herem* against him in his absence, in the heaviest formula of curse the Sephardic tradition possessed.

He had not arrived at this hour out of nothing. Before the *herem*, as a young man, he had already been moving in circles outside his own community. He had been associating with freethinking Christians — Mennonites, and the dissenting group called the Collegiants, who met in private houses and held that no clergy stood between the believer and the text. He had become a student of Franciscus van den Enden, the ex-Jesuit Latinist whose house on the Singel functioned as a center of radical learning, where the new Cartesian philosophy was discussed without the supervision of any church. By the day of the curse the company he kept had already, in the eyes of his elders, declared him.

He did not, by every account that survives, react to the *herem* with any drama. He went on with his day. Within a few months he had moved out of the Jewish quarter and adopted the Latin form of his name; within a few years he had begun grinding lenses for his living and writing the philosophical work that would not be published in his lifetime; within twenty years he was dead at forty-four. He never converted to anything else. He never returned. The day of the *herem* was the day he became what he was for the rest of his life — which was nothing, in the official register of the world, and was Spinoza, in the register of the mind.

I want to know what that day was like for him. What he did in the morning, where he was when the curse was being read, what he ate, whom he saw, what he was working on. I want what shifted in his body, if anything, when the bell in the Westerkerk a few streets over rang the hour. I do not want what he later said in the *Theological-Political Treatise* and the unpublished apologia and the *Ethics*. I want the man before any of those texts existed. I want the twenty-three-year-old in a small room, on the second-warmest day of the Amsterdam summer, deciding to continue with his afternoon. I want what happened in his hands.

I will not get it. Whatever he felt that day he kept to himself. The biographers who knew him do not record his afternoon. Probably, I suspect, he felt free. But I admit that this is my own prejudice — my own disposition for a life with its own spiritual register, drawn from one's own reading and one's own thinking, without intermediaries.

This is the white space the literary imagination is allowed to enter, on the disciplined terms I will enforce on myself. I will not invent events the record contradicts. I will not put him where he was not. I will, within the door the record leaves open, attempt to be in the room with him. That is what the writing is for.

I begin tomorrow. I do not expect to convert at the end of the inquiry. I do not expect to remain unchanged either. The building is a converted warehouse on the Houtgracht. The day is the second-warmest day of the summer of 1656. The man in the room is twenty-three.

His name is Bento.

Figures at the Threshold

Spinoza

Daniel sits at the desk. He has the books out: Steven Nadler, Yirmiyahu Yovel, the Letters in the Penguin selection, the Wolfson on the Latin terms, the small bound copy of the *herem* text in Portuguese with the English facing translation that he ordered from the Ets Haim library in Amsterdam two months ago. He has been reading for three weeks. He has decided, after all the reading, that the chapter will not stage the day of the *herem* as the day of the conversion. The conversion happened earlier, and silently, and in private rooms.

Bento on the morning of July 27, 1656 is not converting. He has converted. He converted, in the only sense that matters for a thinking man, over four years in van den Enden's study reading Descartes; over several Sundays among the Collegiants meeting in private houses outside the formal congregations; over many nights in his own bed working out what could and could not be said about the Hebrew Bible if one read it the way van den Enden had taught him to read Cicero. The day of the *herem* is the day the community catches up with him. The drama of the day is the drama of a public form arriving at an interior that has already finished with it.

This is what releases the chapter for Daniel. There is no scene at the synagogue. There is no climax. The day, on the page, must be quiet, because the day, in fact, was quiet. The community did the loud thing. Bento did not.

He opens the manuscript. He writes a date at the top of the page: *27 July 1656.* He begins.

{

• • •

}

He woke at the usual hour, in the room above what had been his father's establishment, to the sound of carts on the wet stones of the Houtgracht below. The summer had been warm and the air at the open window smelled, as it always did in July, of canal water and of pitch from the shipyards on the IJ. He washed his face from the bowl. He stood for a moment with the towel in his hand and looked at the window without seeing through it. The previous night Jarig Jelles had come to find him at the bookseller's near the Rokin and had told him, quietly, in Dutch — Jelles spoke Dutch, not Portuguese; he was a spice-merchant from one of the Mennonite families and he had no Portuguese — that the *herem* would be pronounced in the morning. The elders had come close to issuing it once or twice in the past months and had drawn back. They were not drawing back now. Jelles had asked whether he could walk with him back to the Houtgracht. Bento had said it was not necessary.

He had decided some weeks earlier not to attend. To attend would be to acknowledge that the form was addressed to him.

He had, in his own mind, acknowledged nothing. The ceremony had nothing to do with him.

He sat down at the small table. There were three books on it: a Cicero in the Plantin edition van den Enden had lent him last winter; a Hebrew Bible his father had given him on his thirteenth birthday and which he kept open at Genesis; a copy of Descartes's *Principia Philosophiae* that he had bought from a Dutch printer who had been amused that a Portuguese Jew was buying it. Beside the books were a pen, an inkwell, and a sheet on which he had been working out — in the Latin that had become, over four years, the language in which he could think most precisely — a problem of his own; a paragraph; the beginning of an inquiry into what could be said about the affects after Descartes, whose treatment of the passions Bento found at once indispensable and, in some way he could not yet name, wrong. The sheet had been waiting since the afternoon of the day before yesterday. He looked at it. He did not pick up the pen.

He was twenty-three. He was slight, dark, with the pallor of a young man who had done less of his living in the open air than he should have. The household he had been born into had been emptying for as long as he could remember. His mother Hanna had died of consumption when he was six. His older brother Isaac had died at twenty-two, in 1649, when Bento was sixteen, after a short illness no one had been able to name. His stepmother Esther had died in 1653, of the same kind of unnamed wasting. His father Michael had followed her in March 1654, two years and four months ago, of a complication of the lungs the physician had said was probably of long standing. Each death had taken from the table one of the people who would have asked after Bento's day. The remaining family — his half-sister Rebecca, his brother-in-law Samuel — were no longer at the table. They had become his adversaries in the inheritance suit. It had been the proper business of the *bet din* to settle that suit. He had taken it to the Dutch.

He had been raised to be a merchant. He had been one for two years after his father died. The business had failed in his hands; he had not been very interested in it. Two months ago he had appeared in the Dutch civil court — not the *bet din*, not the community's own tribunal — to settle the inheritance dispute with his half-sister Rebecca. He had won. He had taken from the Dutch judges the legal claim he was entitled to, and then he had, as he had planned to, given most of it back to her, keeping only what he needed: a few sums, the books from his father's library that interested him, a small stipend that would not last forever. The choice of the Dutch court rather than the *bet din* had been remarked on. The community had understood it for what it was. He had been showing them, before they showed him, that he was no longer one of theirs.

He picked up the pen. He wrote one sentence. He read it. He crossed it out. He did not write another. He pushed the chair back, stood up, took his hat from the peg by the door, and went down the stair.

{

• • •

}

The Houtgracht was alive with the morning. Servants going to the bakers; a fish-cart from the Damrak; two women in the dark Spanish dress that the older Sephardim still wore for the markets, carrying baskets, talking in the Portuguese his mother had spoken to him as a child, before she died when he was six. He greeted no one. No one greeted him. He had not been formally separated yet — that, he knew, would be done within the hour — but the elders had signalled for some weeks that the community was not to engage with him casually. The greetings had stopped two months ago. He had noticed the stopping the way one notices weather. It was a fact. It did not require a response.

He walked toward the Singel. He was going to van den Enden's. It was the only place in the city he wanted to be on this morning.

Franciscus van den Enden was fifty-four. He had been a Jesuit and had left the Order; he had been, briefly, a soldier; he was now a bookseller, a Latinist, the keeper of a school for the sons of certain Amsterdam merchants who wanted their boys taught Latin in the way the Jesuits had taught it without being taught Catholicism alongside it. He had been teaching Bento Latin for nearly four years. The Latin had progressed faster than he had expected. They had moved through Terence and Cicero; they had begun, in the last six months, to read Descartes, on whom van den Enden would not commit himself but on whom Bento had begun to feel — very privately; he had said nothing of this to anyone — that he could write a small commentary if he had the time and the place. They read in Latin. They argued in Latin. The arguing, in van den Enden's house, was the point. Van den Enden had taught Bento, in the way Bento had not been taught at the Talmud Torah, that there was no text whose authority could not be questioned by an attentive reader.

The walk to the Singel was twenty minutes. He went by the Houtmarkt — the timber market, where the great loose piles of pine and oak from the Baltic gave the air the resin smell he had loved since he was a child — and he turned north along the Geldersekade until it joined the Damrak; he crossed the Dam, where the burghers were already at the steps of the new Town Hall doing whatever they did at that hour; and he turned west into the smaller streets toward the Singel canal. The bell tower of the Westerkerk, which was the tallest in the city, was visible above the rooftops to his left. The bell would ring nine soon. The *herem*, he believed, would be pronounced at the third hour by the Jewish reckoning, which was — counting from sunrise on a midsummer morning in Amsterdam — somewhere close to nine in the Christian.

He arrived at van den Enden's door and knocked.

{

• • •

}

Van den Enden opened it himself. He was in shirt-sleeves; he had ink on his right hand; he had been working at his desk. He saw Bento and he understood what the day was. He said, in Latin: *Entra, Benedicte.* He had been calling him *Benedictus* — the Latin form — for two years, whether they were alone or with company. It was one of the small private signals between them that they had not discussed. Bento had registered it. He had not used the form himself, yet.

He went in. The house was narrow and tall, like all the canal-houses; the front room was the bookshop, low-ceilinged, with its presses and its shelves that had not been dusted in a long time; the back room, up a half-flight of stairs, was van den Enden's study. The morning light came in from the canal-side window. There was a copy of the *Principia Philosophiae* open on the table, marked at the second part. There was a Spanish Bible. There was, surprisingly, a copy of the Hebrew Bible — van den Enden did not read Hebrew, but he kept it because Bento had been reading from it aloud and translating, and van den Enden had been interrupting with the kinds of philological questions that the rabbis at the Talmud Torah had taught Bento not to ask out loud, and that van den Enden enjoyed asking precisely because the rabbis had taught Bento not to ask them.

Van den Enden did not mention the *herem.* They sat. He poured the small bitter coffee that he had begun importing through a Levantine merchant on the Kloveniersburgwal who was, perhaps, the only person in the city able to find decent beans. They began where they had left off two days before — a passage in the *Principia,* the second part, the section on motion. Descartes had argued that rest was a positive condition, an *aliquid positivum,* not the mere absence of motion. Bento was not persuaded. *Si requies est aliquid positivum,* he said — if rest is something positive — *cur tunc requiritur causa ad ipsam tollendam, et nulla ad ipsam producendam?* If rest were positive, why should one need a cause to remove it and no cause to produce it? Van den Enden made his usual noises — the half-grunt, the *hmm,* the soft Latin protest. He said Descartes had not in fact argued the absence of cause for rest, only its self-sufficiency once present. Bento said the distinction was not real. They went on. The argument worked itself, in van den Enden's house, the way arguments did — Bento setting the question, van den Enden complicating it, Bento accepting the complication and using it to set the next question.

The small argument about rest was the surface. Behind it ran the larger argument Bento had been carrying out in his own mind for months. He had taken from Descartes — and through van den Enden's house from the larger Cartesian project — the conviction that philosophy could and should be built the way Euclid built geometry: from definitions through axioms to demonstrated propositions, in an order so strict that no link in the chain could be honestly denied. The method, he had come to think, was right. What he was beginning to think wrong was where Descartes had stopped. Descartes had divided substance into two — thought and extension, mind and body — and had then spent the rest of his work trying to bridge a gap his own division had created. The division, Bento had begun to suspect, was unnecessary. There was, when one looked carefully, only one substance, of which thought and extension were two attributes. The conclusion was not yet his to demonstrate; he had just begun to write Latin paragraphs of his own; the *quod erat demonstrandum* of his own *Ethics* lay nearly twenty years in the future. But the instinct of it was firm. He had taken Descartes's method and was preparing, without yet having said so to anyone in the room, to use the method to overturn Descartes's conclusion.

They had been at it for forty minutes when the bell of the Westerkerk struck.

It struck nine times. Bento counted the strikes without intending to. After the ninth he sat with the pen still in his hand and listened to the silence after the bell.

Van den Enden did not look up from the page. He made one of the small grunts. He said, in Dutch — he switched, deliberately, into Dutch — *Het is nu klaar. Da is gedaan.* The Dutch and the Latin ran together in his mouth as they often did. *Now it is finished. The thing is done.*

Bento did not answer immediately. He put the pen down. He sat for a moment with his hands flat on the table.

He said, in Dutch: *Ja. Het is nu klaar.*

Yes. It is finished.

They went back to the *Principia.* Van den Enden was already speaking. The hour passed.

{

• • •

}

He left van den Enden's house at eleven. The bell of the Westerkerk had rung twice more by then. The canal water had begun to glitter under the higher sun. The day was going to be warm. He had a small errand at the bookseller's near the Rokin — he wanted to know whether a copy of the Maimonides Latin selection had come in, the small Buxtorf edition that one of the Hamburg houses had been promising — and he walked south toward it.

The streets were full. Amsterdam at the high point of the morning, the stalls in the squares loud, the men on the canals shouting from boat to boat in their flat broad Dutch. He passed through it as someone who had lived in this city all his life and had not, today, become a different person inside it. The *herem* had been pronounced; the curse had been read; the hall on the Houtgracht had heard the formula and the candles had been extinguished one after another. None of this had reached the squares. The squares did not know. The man with the eel cart at the Nieuwmarkt did not know that one of the Portuguese had been thrown out by his elders; the woman selling small almond cakes at the Damrak did not know it; the burgher at the Town Hall steps did not know it. The Amsterdam that surrounded Bento as he walked did not know what the elders thought it must mean for him to have done what he had done.

He arrived at the bookseller. The Maimonides had not come in. The bookseller — a Dutchman, a Mennonite, married to an Englishwoman, kind, slow to speak — invited him to stay for a cup of tea. Bento accepted. They sat in the back room. The bookseller's wife brought the tea in a small English pot. They talked about a sermon that the bookseller had heard the previous Sunday at the Collegiant meeting — Bento had been to those meetings several times over the past year, and had met some of the men who came to them — and the bookseller was halfway through a summary of the sermon when the bell of the Westerkerk struck twelve.

Bento listened. He drank the tea. He said nothing about what was happening or had happened in the synagogue half a mile away, and the bookseller and his wife did not know what was happening or had happened, and the conversation continued, and at the bottom of his cup, when he tipped it, was the small dark leaf the English used for telling fortunes. He looked at it and smiled. The bookseller's wife laughed and said she did not know how to read them. He said it was just as well.

He left. He walked home.

He took a route that brought him within a hundred yards of the synagogue building. He had not intended to. He had taken the route automatically; it was the way he had come back from the bookseller's twice a week for years. The building was a converted warehouse, brick, plain, with the small windows of its original commercial use still visible above the door. The front was empty when he passed. The morning's gathering had ended; the men who had come for the *herem* had gone back to their houses or their offices for the midday meal. The door was closed. There was no one on the step. He walked past it without slowing and without looking at it for more than the second it took to register that the door was closed.

{

• • •

}

He returned to the Houtgracht in the early afternoon. The street had thinned — the heat had reached its high point — and he climbed the stair. The room was warmer than it had been when he left it. He sat at the table. The sheet of paper was where he had left it. The two crossed-out sentences from the morning were still on it. He looked at them for a moment. He picked up the pen and wrote another sentence. Then another. The second sentence followed from the first, which was what mattered. Then a third. Then he put the pen down and closed his eyes.

He thought. He did not pray; he had never prayed, in any tradition; the form of address that prayer assumed was not available to him. He thought in the way he had been thinking for several years, which was the slow examination of a structure whose elements he had not yet fully named.

He thought about what had been done to him that morning. He thought about the men who had done it. Morteira, who had taught him for ten years and had loved him and had wept, two months ago, when the question of the *herem* had first come formally before the elders; Morteira had pleaded with him then, privately, to make any small gesture of repentance, any small public acknowledgement, that would let the elders close the matter without the formal curse, and Bento had thanked him and had declined. Morteira had not wept again. By this morning Morteira would have been one of the men reading the formula. Aboab da Fonseca, the chief rabbi, whose voice was always the loudest in any room and whose Hebrew was the most polished and whose authority was the least secure — Aboab would have given the matter the rhetorical weight he always gave such matters. The *parnassim* — the elders, the lay leaders — would have sat in their chairs along the front bench and would have nodded at the appropriate moments. The community in the body of the hall would have stood in silence. The candles would have been lit at the start and would have been put out one by one by the *shamash* as the formula went on. He had been present, several years before, at the *herem* of another man, a Spaniard from Madrid whose name he could not now remember; he knew what the form looked like.

He did not feel angry with Morteira. He did not, on examination, feel anything that he would have called an emotion in the sense the schoolmen had described. He felt — and the word for it, in the Latin he was beginning to think in, would have been *intelligo*, an understanding rather than a feeling — that what had happened to him this morning had been inevitable, and that the only question that had been open was whether he would help them by attending or oblige them to do it without him. He had chosen the latter. He had been correct to choose it. It had spared them nothing and it had spared him a humiliation that was not necessary to the philosophical position.

The philosophical position, of course, was the question. He had begun to see, in the last several months, that the position would have to be set out in some kind of order — not yet a treatise, perhaps; perhaps only a long letter to himself; but in order. The questions were too many to hold in his head. He had begun to draft, in the back of one of the Cicero notebooks, a list of the propositions he would need to set out, and the order in which they would have to follow each other; he had crossed most of them out and tried again; he had crossed most of those out and tried again. He had, in the last week, begun to wonder whether the geometric form — the form of Euclid, the *quod erat demonstrandum* — might be the only form rigorous enough to hold what he needed to say.

The center of it, when he tried to find the center, was always the same. Substance. There was, he was beginning to think, only one of it. What the schoolmen called God and what the natural philosophers called nature were not two things, they were two names for the same thing, and the appearance that they were two was a confusion produced by the limited way human beings perceived their own situation inside the substance they were a part of. The thought was very large. It was also, when he held it carefully, very simple. It was the thought that — if he were ever to articulate it; if he were ever to set it out in proper order — would explain why the *herem* this morning, with its formula about the apostate and the heretic and the pursuer of foreign gods, had no purchase on him. There were no foreign gods. There was no apostasy. There was only the substance, which had no inside and no outside, no chosen people and no rejected people, no covenant and no curse. The community had pronounced its formula in good faith, in the language it had inherited, against a man it correctly understood to be no longer one of them. He had, however, by the time the formula had been pronounced, ceased to be the kind of being to whom the formula could be addressed. They had cursed an apostate. He was not an apostate. He was simply elsewhere, in a country whose existence they did not yet know about and which he himself had only begun to map.

He opened his eyes. The light had shifted. The afternoon was tilting toward evening.

He stood. He went to the small chest where he kept the few things he had decided to take with him when he left the Houtgracht — and he had decided to leave; the question was only whether in a week, a month, or a season — and he opened it. There was little inside. A change of linen. A second pair of shoes. The Cicero notebook. The packet of his father's letters that he had not yet been able to throw away. He closed the chest.

He went back to the table. He picked up the pen.

{

• • •

}

The bell of the Westerkerk struck six. He had filled half a sheet. The Latin was better than it had been in the morning; the morning had been blocked, the afternoon had moved, and the argument had, for the first time in two days, taken a shape he could see ahead. He put the pen down. He stood. He stretched his shoulders, which had stiffened.

He went to the window. The canal below was quiet now — the working day was ending — and the air over the water was still warm. He could see, between the houses opposite, a small slice of the western sky, which was taking on the color of the second-warmest evening of the summer. Below his window a child was playing with a wooden hoop, alone, rolling it between her two small hands and chasing it for a few steps when it veered. Her mother was sitting on the step of the door across the street, watching her, paying no attention to the upstairs window of the house across from hers. Bento watched the child for some time. The hoop caught a stone and the child stooped to pick it up.

He turned from the window. He went down the stair. He had not eaten since the bread and coffee at van den Enden's. He went out into the street. The street was half-empty in the late light. He walked a little. He passed the door of a house that belonged to a cousin of his late stepmother — and the cousin, who happened to be at the door, saw him, and looked at him with the look that Bento had been seeing in the eyes of the community for some weeks now, except that today the look had sharpened and become final. The cousin did not speak. The cousin stepped back into the doorway and closed the door.

Bento continued. He bought, from a stall at the corner, a piece of bread and a small piece of cheese. He sat on the low wall that ran along the canal and ate. The water was dark now under the deepening sky. A few boats passed; the boatmen did not look at him; he was, by all the formal measures of the world he had been raised in, no longer present.

He finished the cheese. He stood. He walked back to the house. He climbed the stair. He went into the room. He did not light a candle. He sat at the table in the gathering dark.

He had all the time in the world now. It was what the morning had given him. He had become, in the small hours of this single day, a man with no community and no church and no obligation to anyone but himself and his work. He was twenty-three. The work, which had been inside him as an unformed pressure for several years, could now begin to take its shape outside him. He could not yet see what shape it would take. He did not need to see it tonight. He had time.

The bell of the Westerkerk struck seven.

{

• • •

}

Daniel sets the manuscript aside. He has written more than he had planned to write today. The light at the north window has gone bluer; it is past five. He stands. He stretches his shoulders, which have stiffened in the same place Bento's stiffened in the chapter.

From the apartment, even at this height, he can hear the sirens — the fire trucks on Lexington Avenue, the New York note that arrives at any hour and at any floor. He goes to the hall window. Lexington at this hour is a yellow river along the upper blocks, converting to red along the lower, the taillights of the cars all running downtown together.

He thinks the day is right. Bento on the morning of July 27, 1656 was not turning. He had turned. The community was the one doing something on that day, not Bento. Bento was, in a sense the lawyer in Daniel finds satisfying, simply the addressee of a notice that confirmed a legal status he had already brought about by his own actions over several years. The Dutch court two months earlier had been the first public act; the herem was the second. The first he had instigated. The second he had not had to.

What strikes Daniel as he closes the page is the quietness of the day. He had expected, before he sat down to write, that the chapter would have to find some form of climax — some interior storm, some scene of inward struggle. The reading had not supported it. The record showed, as far as one could read it, that Bento had not struggled on that day. He had drunk coffee with van den Enden. He had walked to a bookseller. He had eaten bread and cheese on a wall by the canal. He had filled half a sheet with Latin. The drama of the day had been the drama of an absence — of the great event the community had meant to inflict on him having simply not landed where it was aimed. Bento had been somewhere else by then. He had been there for two years.

Daniel knows Part III of the *Ethics* the way a constitutional lawyer knows the Bill of Rights — from many readings over many years, with marginal annotations that have accumulated in three colors of ink, each color the residue of a different decade. Spinoza in the *Ethics* defined the affects, the *affectus*, the modifications of the body's power to act, and gave a list of forty-eight of them, each derived in order from the three primary affects of joy, sadness, and desire. Daniel, thinking about Bento on the wall by the canal eating bread and cheese, wonders which of the forty-eight Bento would have selected if asked, fifteen years later, to name what he had felt on July 27, 1656. *Acquiescentia in se ipso* — self-contentment, the joy that arises from the contemplation of one's own power of acting — would have been on the list. *Securitas* — security, the joy that arises from a future contemplated without fear — would have been on it. *Animositas* — strength of mind, the desire by which one preserves one's own being from the dictates of reason alone — almost certainly. Not anger. Not vengeance. Not contempt. The negative affects in the *Ethics* are the affects of the man whose understanding is incomplete. Bento in the room in the dark would have understood enough.

What Daniel finds, when he sits with the chapter, is something he had not expected to find when he began. He has been validated by writing it. Bento at twenty-three on the evening of the *herem* was an individual, not a member of a community, no longer a member of his religion, not yet a member of any other; he was a loose participant in a city and a country whose rules were semi-tolerant; he had no party, no movement, no church, no club. Daniel at seventy-eight, three centuries and an ocean later, is in an analogous position. He has no party. He has no movement. He has no church. He has no club. He lives in a country in an era of tolerance with rights — and the rights, the ones in the small paperback he occasionally carries, were drafted in part by men who had read Spinoza. He is, in his own quiet way, near the position Bento was in on the wall by the canal in 1656. The resemblance is not identity. The resemblance is enough.

Daniel closes the notebook. He looks at the photograph on the bookshelf to his right — the man in the tallit, the unidentifiable face, the darkened print in the Art Nouveau frame. The man in the photograph would have lived in some country and some century in which the *herem* of 1656 was a known fact, transmitted in the family's silence rather than its speech, the way most facts of consequence are transmitted in such families.

He stands. He goes to make coffee.

Figures at the Threshold

Pascal

Daniel sits at the desk. The Pascal materials are laid out: the *Pensées* in the Pléiade edition, the older Brunschvicg edition for comparison; the *Provinciales*; the small bound facsimile of the *Mémorial* — the parchment Pascal sewed into the lining of his coat and which a servant found only after his death — published with a critical apparatus he has been working through for two weeks; Gilberte Périer's *Vie de Pascal*; the Krailsheimer essays.

He has been thinking about the difference between Pascal and Spinoza. Both men, intelligent past the standard of their age, in the formative years of their twenties and early thirties, in the same century, separated by nine hundred kilometers and two religious traditions — both at the moment of a decisive turn that altered the rest of their lives. The difference is the directionality.

Spinoza's turn was outward and conceptual. He had moved, across years, toward a position from which his community had to expel him. The *herem* caught up with what he had already done. The day of the curse was the day his interior became externally visible. He left no record of the day itself; the elders left the curse; he wrote, eventually, the *Ethics*.

Pascal's turn was inward and immediate. Two hours, on a Monday in November, between half past ten and half past midnight. He recorded it himself, in the heat of the experience, on a sheet of paper he later transcribed onto a parchment, and the parchment he sewed into the lining of his coat. It went with him for eight years, undetected by anyone, until he died and the servant found it.

There is no question, in Pascal's case, of whether the moment happened. The document is in the Bibliothèque nationale; Daniel has seen photographs of it; the handwriting, the abbreviations, the smudges, the second draft on parchment — all of it survives. There is, however, the question of what happened. The text of the *Mémorial* is not a description; it is an emission. Words and phrases pour out without syntax: FEU, Certitude, Joie, Paix, the names of God, fragments of Latin. The text records a man undergoing something with a depth of conviction Daniel finds unsettling.

The lawyer in him reads the document and does what the lawyer does. He asks what the testimony shows and what it does not. The *Mémorial* shows that on November 23, 1654, Pascal experienced something he understood as the direct presence of God. It does not show that God was present. It does not show, alternatively, that anything else was present. It shows what Pascal, immediately afterward and persistently for eight years, believed. The lawyer's discipline cannot adjudicate the question of what was actually there. The lawyer's discipline can only describe.

Daniel has decided to enter the night carefully, in the language of the body and the room, and to trust the reader to read the experience through that.

He opens the manuscript. He writes a date at the top of the page: *23 November 1654.*

{

• • •

}

He was thirty-one. He had, in the world's reckoning, succeeded — the calculating machine, the work on the cycloid, the correspondence with Fermat that had founded a new branch of mathematics, the small reputation already settled around his name in the Académie of Mersenne and beyond. He had also been ill. The illnesses were various and chronic; he had been told, by physicians who could do nothing for him, to vary his life and amuse himself, and he had taken the advice. For two years he had moved among the Parisian salons — the rooms in which the leading thinkers of the city discussed love, morals, and philosophy in front of women who, in many cases, presided over the conversation with more rigor than the men did; he had played dice and ombre; he had spent evenings in the houses of the duke this and the marquise that. He had not enjoyed it, exactly. He had observed it. He had begun, in the last months, to write down small thoughts about what he was observing — fragments on a sheet at the back of a notebook, returned to in the early mornings — that he was not yet calling anything but that, much later, would end in the unfinished apology for Christianity that nobody saw in his lifetime and that everyone would call the *Pensées*.

The fragments that interested him most concerned the foundations of authority and the nature of the human creature who submits to it. He had been reading Hobbes. He had been thinking, in the manner of Hobbes but in his own French Catholic frame, that political order does not rest on justice or on moral virtue but on force, custom, and the imagination. Custom was what made the present arrangement seem natural; imagination was what kept the population from looking too closely at what custom concealed; force was the residual, available when the other two failed. The ruler who governed by these three was not, in any straightforward sense, just; he was, however, effective, and effectiveness was the most that could be expected from human institutions, given what human beings were. What human beings were, Pascal had come to think, was fallen — self-deceiving, divided against themselves, in need of constraint. The cheerfulness of the salons was a kind of group denial of this fact. The seriousness of Port-Royal was the only institution he had encountered that took the fact seriously.

He lived alone in an apartment in the Faubourg Saint-Jacques, with two servants and a housekeeper. His older sister Gilberte was in Clermont with her husband Florin Périer and their children. His younger sister Jacqueline was at Port-Royal des Champs, three years a nun, and corresponded with him in letters that had become more and more direct.

The relationship with Jacqueline was the longest unfinished argument of his life. They had been close in childhood, closer than either had been to Gilberte; she had nursed him through the worst of the illnesses of his twenties; she had written poetry that the queen had read; she had then, against the wishes of their father and against his own quieter wishes, decided to enter Port-Royal as a *postulante* in 1652, weeks after their father's death, when the household was at its most fragile. He had resisted her vows. He had written her letters of considerable length. He had pleaded, as his father would have pleaded, that the family had a claim on her. She had refused the claim. She had taken her vows in 1653. He had given her the dowry the convent required. He had also, for some months, ceased to speak to her, and had then resumed speaking to her, and had then, slowly, allowed her to write to him about his soul.

She wrote about his soul as if she were writing a brief. She told him plainly that he was wasting himself in the world. She told him that the salons were a poor substitute for the only thing that mattered. She told him that he was, under the surface of the wit and the mathematics and the calculating machine, a man with religious questions he had been refusing to ask. He wrote back politely. He had no intention of making a retreat at Port-Royal. He had attended the Easter services there in the spring and had felt what one always felt in the chapel at Port-Royal — a kind of cold seriousness — and had left feeling that the place was not for him.

He had been ill for the past month. The headaches had been worse. The pain in his teeth had been worse. He had been sleeping poorly. There had been, ten weeks earlier, an incident on the Pont de Neuilly: the carriage, the horses, the broken traces, the moment of the lead pair going over the side of the bridge while the equipage stopped at the lip. He had not been hurt. He had walked back to the apartment afterward without speaking. He did not regard the incident as a sign. Voltaire, three generations later, would say that Pascal's piety was the consequence of fear after the bridge. Voltaire would be wrong. The bridge had not made him afraid; the bridge had only made him notice that he was, like everyone else, mortal, and the noticing had not been a revelation.

What had been changing in him over the autumn was something

quieter than fear. He had begun to find the salons hollow. He had found his own conversation — when he replayed it in his head walking home — hollow. He had not been able to read mathematics with his old pleasure. He had been reading, instead, the Old Testament, slowly, in the Vulgate, and the *Confessions* of Augustine in a Latin edition with the small annotations of a previous owner that he had begun to grow fond of. Antoine Singlin at Port-Royal had recommended the *Confessions* through Jacqueline a year and a half ago and Pascal had not gotten around to them until October. Augustine had moved him in a way that pure mathematics no longer did. He had not yet admitted this to anyone, including himself.

This was the man who sat at the desk in the apartment in the Faubourg Saint-Jacques on the evening of Monday, November 23, 1654, the day of Saint Clement, pope and martyr.

{

• • •

}

The desk faced a window. The window faced the small interior court of the building, which was dark. There was a single candle lit, set in a brass holder his sister Gilberte had given him when he had moved into the apartment. The candle had burned down by perhaps a quarter. Beside the candle were a sheet of paper, an inkwell, a quill, and two books: the Vulgate, open to the Psalms, and the *Confessions* in the small Latin edition.

He did not at first realize anything was changing. He had been reading the *Confessions* for an hour. He had reached Book Eight, which was the chapter in which Augustine described his own conversion in the garden in Milan. Pascal had read this passage many times. He had always read it with a small intellectual interest — Augustine the rhetorician describing the rhetoric of his own experience — and a small reserve. The reserve was the residue of the philosopher's habit. One did not, as a serious reader, accept an author's account of a transforming experience at face value. One asked what work the experience was doing in the text.

Tonight the reserve had not held. He had reached the passage in which Augustine, in the garden at Milan, hears the voice of the child — *tolle, lege; tolle, lege* — and opens the volume of Saint Paul to the verse about putting on the Lord Jesus Christ. He had read the passage. He had stopped. He had put his finger on the page to keep his place, but he had not wanted to keep his place; he had not wanted to read on. Something in the room had become attentive.

He looked up from the book. The candle was steady. The court outside the window was dark. There was no sound from the street; it was past ten; the Faubourg was quiet. He could hear his own breath. He could hear the small ticking of the wood of the desk as it settled in the cooling air.

The bell of Saint-Étienne-du-Mont, two streets over, struck the half-hour. Half past ten.

He sat without moving. He was aware, in a way he had not been aware before — in a way he had not known one could be aware of — that the small motions of his attention were preparing themselves for something he could not yet describe. He had spent his life examining the precise mechanics of attention. He had written, in a fragment that would later be in the *Pensées*, that the proper conduct of attention was the foundation of all rigorous thought. He had not, however, been prepared for the kind of attention that was, at this moment, organizing itself in him toward a point he had not yet seen.

He did not move. He did not pick up the quill. He did not put down the book. He sat with his finger on the page, and he listened.

Then it began.

{

• • •

}

It came as fire. He understood immediately, without forming the thought, that this was not a metaphor. There was no fire in the room. The candle was steady; the wood of the desk was cool to his hand; nothing had ignited; nothing was burning. The fire was inside him. It was inside him at the level the schoolmen had called the heart — but the schoolmen's heart was a metaphor, a placeholder for the seat of the will; this was no metaphor. There was a fire in his chest. It rose from the chest into the throat, from the throat into the head; it moved through him as if his body were a flue and the fire were a wind.

He did not feel pain. He felt heat, but the heat was not damaging. It was, he understood without forming the thought, a heat that purified rather than consumed.

The first thing he experienced inside the heat was certainty. Not a logical certainty; not the certainty of a demonstrated proposition; not the certainty of mathematics, which he knew. A different certainty. The certainty that there was something there. Something not himself. Something not the room, not the candle, not the books, not the silence. Something that was, in a way he could not have explained but did not need to explain, simply *there*, with a presence so dense that the entire interior of the apartment had become organized around it.

He understood, at that moment, that the something was God. He did not arrive at the understanding by argument. The understanding was given. The God of Abraham, of Isaac, of Jacob — this had been the formula his eye had rested on a few hours before in the Vulgate, in a passage of Exodus he had not been reading on purpose — *that* God. Not the abstract God of the proofs. Not the God of the philosophers and the scholars; not the *primum movens* of Aristotle, not the *res cogitans et extensa* of Descartes, not the geometrical God who somewhere in Amsterdam, at this same hour, a young man named Bento was beginning to articulate. The God of the patriarchs. The personal God. The God who had spoken from the bush. The God who had, at this moment, in the apartment in the Faubourg Saint-Jacques, declared himself in the form of fire.

He began to weep. He did not realize he was weeping until the tears had been on his face for some seconds. He was not weeping in grief. He was weeping in a state for which he had no word; the closest word, when he found it later in the Vulgate, would be *gaudium* — joy — but the word as it stood in the Latin was inadequate; the joy at this moment was an ocean and the word was a cup.

He understood, also, that he had been separated from this God. That the entire course of his life — the brilliance, the mathematics, the salons, the gambling, the careful conversations, even the slow honest reading of Augustine in October and November — had been a separation. He had been somewhere else. The somewhere else had not been hostile to God; it had simply not been God. He had been wandering, in a country whose existence he had not denied but whose direction he had not faced, and now he had been made to face it.

He whispered, in Latin, the verse from the Psalm he had been reading earlier in the afternoon: *Non obliviscar sermones tuos.* I will not forget your words.

The bell of Saint-Étienne-du-Mont struck eleven.

The fire continued. It did not lessen. He sat with the tears running, with his hands flat on the desk, with the candle steady, with the book open at the passage about Augustine in the garden, and he was inside something he could not have produced and could not have prevented and could not now leave.

He lost track of time. He understood that time had become a different kind of substance from the substance it had been at half past ten.

Phrases formed in him without his choosing them. They came in fragments. *Certitude. Sentiment. Joie. Paix.* He did not know whether he was speaking the words or whether they were arising in his mind as words without sound. He had the sense that the difference did not matter. *Dieu de Jésus-Christ.* He had been a Christian since infancy; he had been baptized; he had been confirmed; he had attended the Mass with his sisters and his father all his life; but now, for the first time, the formula *Dieu de Jésus-Christ* meant something he had not previously known it could mean. Christ was not a doctrine. Christ was a person. Christ was the means by which the God of fire had become approachable; Christ was the bridge that he had not previously understood he had been crossing every time he had said *Pater noster* without thinking.

He thought, with a clarity that surprised him: *I have separated myself from him.*

He thought: *Mon Dieu, me quitterez-vous?* My God, will you leave me?

The thought of the question opened in him a dread that the joy could not keep out. The dread was that the experience would end and that, when it ended, he would be returned to the country he had been wandering in, and that he would lose what he had been given, and that he would not be given it again.

He found that he was praying. He did not know that he had begun to pray. The prayer was the only available response to the dread. *Que je n'en sois jamais séparé.* Let me never be separated from him.

The bell struck twelve.

He had been inside the experience for an hour and a half. The experience continued.

He understood that he had to take this with him into his life. That he had to renounce — *renonciation totale et douce* — the country of the salons and the gambling and the indifferent Christianity. That he had to submit himself to a director, a real director, at Port-Royal, the way Jacqueline had been telling him for two years that he should. That he had to write down, immediately and exactly, what was happening, so that when it ended he would not lose the shape of it.

The fire began, around half past midnight, to recede.

It did not vanish. It withdrew. It moved, by some measure he could not see, from the foreground of his interior to the background; it became a pressure he could carry rather than a presence that filled him. He was given back to himself. He was, at half past midnight on November 23 (now November 24) of the year of grace 1654, alone in the apartment in the Faubourg Saint-Jacques, with the candle still steady, the wood of the desk still cool, the book still open, and tears still on his face that he had not yet wiped.

The bell of Saint-Étienne-du-Mont struck the half hour.

He picked up the quill.

{

• • •

}

He had a sheet of paper. He began to write.

He did not write a sentence. He wrote a date. *L'an de grâce 1654. Lundi 23 novembre, jour de saint Clément, pape et martyr.* He named the date because the date was a fact. He wrote *Veille de saint Chrysogone, martyr.* Saint Chrysogonus, whose feast day was the next day, the 24th. The vigil of Saint Chrysogonus. He wrote *Depuis environ dix heures et demie du soir jusques environ minuit et demi.* The hours were facts.

Then he wrote, in capitals, *FEU.*

The capitals were not for emphasis. The capitals were because the lower-case letters were not adequate to the word. The word was the only word that was adequate to what had been in him.

He wrote the names of God. He wrote *Certitude.* He wrote *Joie, joie, joie, pleurs de joie.* He wrote the fragments of Latin and French as they came to him, in the order they came, without syntax, without paragraphs. He understood, while writing, that the document he was making was not a description; it was a record of what could not be described, in a form that reproduced the failure of description; the disjointedness of the page would itself be testimony.

He wrote for some time. He did not know how long. The candle had burned down by another quarter when he put the quill down. The page was full. He read it. He read it twice. He found that the words on the page, while they could not contain the experience, gave him enough purchase on the experience that he believed he would be able to remember it.

He could not, however, trust himself to remember it. He had spent his adult life knowing that the human mind under the pressure of time loses what it has been given. He had written, somewhere in the small thoughts he had been gathering for what would much later be the *Pensées*, that the human condition is a condition of forgetting. He would forget the night. He would lose the fire. The fire would withdraw further; it would, in the long course of the years, become a memory that grew dimmer; it would, perhaps, eventually be re-narrated as something less than it had been. He could not allow this.

He took the page. He folded it in half and then in quarters. He did not throw it in the small fireplace, which had gone cold. He did not put it in the drawer of the desk. He held it in his hand for some minutes.

Within the next several days he would copy the page onto a piece of parchment, more carefully, with the same disjointedness preserved deliberately, and the parchment he would sew, with his own hands, into the lining of his coat. The folded paper version he would keep with the parchment. Both would be there for eight years. He would, several times a year for those eight years, take out the parchment in private and read it, to remind himself of what had happened on this night and to hold himself, by the thinnest of cords, to the renunciation he had committed to in the small hours of November 24, 1654. He would not show the document to anyone. He would not show it to Jacqueline. He would not show it to his director at Port-Royal, when he eventually accepted one. The document was a private fact between him and the God who had given him the fire.

The servant who would find it after his death would not understand at first what it was.

{

• • •

}

In the morning he went to Mass. He went the following week to Port-Royal des Champs and asked, of Antoine Singlin and of his sister, to be received for a retreat. The retreat began in early January 1655 and lasted two weeks. He spoke very little during it. Jacqueline, when she saw him after, told Gilberte in a letter that she had not seen this version of her brother before. She did not say what she meant by *this version*. The letter survives.

He spent the next two and a half years in a discipline that surprised even Jacqueline, who had been telling him for years that he should. He submitted, as the *Mémorial* committed him to submit, to Singlin as his director. He renounced, more or less, the salons, though his renunciations were never as complete as Jacqueline's; he was a public figure in a way she was not, and the public was a debt he could not entirely repudiate.

He wrote the *Provincial Letters* in 1656 and 1657, defending Jansenism against the Jesuits with a wit and a clarity of prose that made him, in the eyes of educated Europe, the leading polemical writer of his generation; the wit was a worldly weapon used in the service of an unworldly position. The letters were anonymous; everyone knew he had written them; the King's confessor wanted them burned and several were. He began the apology for Christianity that he was working on when he died, and that, in its unfinished state, his nephews and Port-Royal would assemble after his death into the *Pensées*. He returned to mathematics one further time, in 1658, when a wager with friends produced his treatise on the cycloid; even then, the work was framed as a brief return rather than a re-entry.

Jacqueline died in October 1661, at thirty-six, of what was probably the same family illness that would take him. He went to her funeral. He did not speak there.

He died on August 19, 1662, at the age of thirty-nine, of a tumor that had grown in his brain and had given him, at the end, a degree of pain that astonished his physicians. He received the last rites. He said, before he died, *que Dieu ne m'abandonne jamais* — let God never abandon me — and then he died.

The servant, going through the coat he had been wearing in his last weeks, felt a stiffness in the lining and called for someone with a knife. The knife found the parchment, and beside it the folded paper that was the original from the night itself, the two pieces sewn together into a small packet against his chest. Gilberte's husband, when he was shown the document the next day, did not at first understand what it was either. He read it through. He read the date. He read *FEU*. He sat down. He put the parchment on the table and laid the paper beside it. He understood, then, that what he was looking at was the only place in the world where what had happened to his brother-in-law on the night of November 23, 1654 had been recorded, and that the recording had been kept, with such complete privacy, for eight years.

That had been eight years after the night.

{

• • •

}

Daniel sets the manuscript aside. The light at the windows has gone fully blue; it is past seven. He has written longer than he had intended. The Pascal chapter has taken from him a different kind of attention than the Spinoza chapter required. The Spinoza chapter was about a man who refused. The Pascal chapter is about a man who was given — or, more precisely, a man who was disposed, searching, and who received what came to him because he had been positioning himself, without knowing it, to receive it.

What Daniel finds himself with, when he closes the page, is a problem he has not solved and does not expect to solve. He does not believe, in any literal sense, that the experience of November 23, 1654 was the direct presence of God. He cannot. The lawyer in him, and the agnostic he has been for seventy-eight years, do not allow it. He believes, however, that something happened that night that Pascal could not account for in any language other than the one he used, and that the experience reorganized the rest of Pascal's life in a way no other account would have predicted from the man Pascal had been on November 22.

The fire was, in some sense, real. What it was the fire of, Daniel cannot say. The lawyer's discipline cannot determine the question. The lawyer's discipline can only describe the testimony — and accept it as testimony, not as interpretation. The interpretation is what the experiencer brings to the experience afterward, and is by its nature subjective. The lawyer does not adjudicate the interpretation. The lawyer records what the witness said.

What Daniel does not believe, and has not believed for a very long time, is that *miracle* is the right name for what happened to Pascal that night. He does not believe in miracles in the form they are usually told — the form in which the laws of the world are suspended for a person who has merited the suspension or whom God has chosen to favor. Stories of miracles are, for Daniel, stories. Some are pious confabulations. Some are the misreading of natural events by witnesses who lacked the categories to describe what they saw. Some are genuine experiences, intense and real to the experiencer, whose linkage to a divine source is a personal interpretation added afterward. The experience is not the miracle. The experience is the experience. The miracle is what the believer does with the experience.

He thinks, while he is closing the books, of the apartment he and Marie-Claire kept in their first years in Washington — Sutton Towers, in the upper Northwest, with a single tall window in the front room, twelve feet high, that looked out across the trees toward the National Cathedral about a mile to the southeast. It was his job to close the curtain before they went to bed. He always did it without turning on the room's lights, because the Cathedral at that hour, with its discreet illumination on the limestone of the spires, was the kind of view one did not interrupt. He would stand for some seconds at the window before drawing the curtain. He had a small joke with Marie-Claire that he was, every night, giving the Almighty a fair opportunity to send a signal. Marie-Claire did not appreciate the joke. He stopped telling it after the first year. He kept the practice. He was at the window every night they lived in that apartment, and the Cathedral never sent a signal, and he closed the curtain, and they went to bed.

What strikes Daniel, reading his own chapter back, is the parallel with Bento he had not anticipated. Both men, at some moment in their early thirties, had become incapable of the abstract God of the philosophers — the God of demonstration, the God of the proofs. Both had reached for something else. Spinoza had reached for the substance, for the one thing that was both God and nature, that needed no demonstration because it was simply what existed. Pascal had reached for the patriarchs and for the Christ on the bridge. The two reached for opposite poles. They were, however, reaching against the same ceiling. The God of the philosophers, by 1654, in two minds at the same time, had become unavailable to a man capable of attention.

Daniel thinks also of what became of Pascal's Jansenism. It was, in its day, an extreme movement — rigorous, austere, grace-centered, suspicious of the easier consolations the Jesuits offered the world — and it was, by the late seventeenth and through the eighteenth century, suppressed: the bull *Unigenitus*, the dispersal of the nuns, the convent of Port-Royal des Champs razed by royal order in 1709 and the bones of its dead disinterred and scattered. As an institutional fact Jansenism mostly disappeared. What survived, here and there, were certain currents of rigorous, grace-centered Catholic spirituality — heirs of the Jansenist seriousness without its name — that continue to recur in the Church's life whenever the cheerful institutional surface needs unsettling. Pascal's *Mémorial*, sewn into a coat for eight years, is in some sense the founding private document of that recurring strain.

Daniel finds, also, that the chapter has tested a small private worry he had brought to the project at the beginning. He had been concerned, in advance, that he would not be able to write a Pascal chapter without either condescending to the experience or sentimentalizing it. He is not a believer; he does not regard the mystical claim as a claim he can credit; the lawyer's discipline does not let him write *and then God appeared to Pascal in the form of fire* as a sentence the chapter affirms. He had also not wished to write, as the eighteenth century wrote, that Pascal had been a hysteric who experienced a fit. The first of those sentences would have been a betrayal of his own mind. The second would have been a betrayal of Pascal's. He had not been sure, before he sat down, that there was a third option. The third option, when he found it, was simply to describe — to describe what Pascal recorded, in the language Pascal recorded it, with the body and the room around the description, and to let the reader stand at the same distance from the experience that Daniel himself stands at. The reader, like Daniel, will not know what was in the room. The reader, like Daniel, will know that something was. Other readers — readers of a different disposition, readers who are themselves believers — may go further and judge that what was in the room was the true divine presence. Daniel respects that judgment. He places it, however, where it belongs: in the mind of the person experiencing it, who must be a believer for the judgment to make sense, and Daniel is not.

What he does not know, and what he is willing to acknowledge to himself in the gathering blue at the windows, is whether he has thereby done the chapter a kind of injustice. Pascal himself would have said, with the certainty that the *Mémorial* preserves, that the third option Daniel has chosen is also a betrayal. Pascal would have said that the discipline of describing the testimony without crediting it is the lawyer's habit applied to a place where the lawyer's habit will not reach. Pascal would have said: you do not adjudicate a fire by describing the heat; you adjudicate it by being burnt. Daniel has not been burnt. He cannot pretend to have been. He can, at most, set down what the testimony shows and trust the reader, who has also not been burnt, to read the testimony with whatever credence the reader's own life has prepared.

Daniel closes the notebook. He looks at the photograph. He goes to the listening chair by the north window. He opens the iPad. He finds, in the Apple Classics application, the recording of Bach's *Saint John Passion* by Raphaël Pichon's Pygmalion ensemble — a recent recording, by a group he has been following for several years and that has in his ear the right tension between rigor and feeling for this particular work. He sets the volume modestly. The apartment is quiet. The German Lutheran rendering of the *Passio* is a strange counterpoint to the French Catholic mystical fragment he has just spent the day inside, but the strange counterpoint is a fact of his ear and he has stopped questioning it. He listens. The opening chorus begins — *Herr, unser Herrscher* — and the two hours of the work, beginning and ending in the lower strings, will take him to the end of the evening.

Figures at the Threshold

Heine

Daniel sits at the desk. The Heine materials are out: the *Säkularausgabe* in green cloth, the Pléiade French selection he prefers for the prose, the small bound volume of *Briefe an Moses Moser* from the Heine-Institut in Düsseldorf, Sammons's biography, Prawer's monograph on Heine's Jewish material. He has been thinking about Heine for ten days.

Heine is the formal counterpoint to Pascal. Where Pascal converted with the entire weight of an interior experience — the fire that left him weeping at his desk for two hours — Heine converted with the certainty that no interior experience was involved. Where Pascal's conversion was given, Heine's was bought. He is the third figure in the book and, as Daniel has come to see while preparing the chapter, the figure who set the form for everything in modern Western religious life that came after — the modern conversion, the transactional one, the conversion the convert himself does not believe in.

Daniel has been reading the letters to Moses Moser in particular. Moser was Heine's closest friend. They had been students together in Berlin, members together of the short-lived Verein für

Cultur und Wissenschaft der Juden, the Society for the Culture and Science of the Jews. The Society had been founded in 1819 by Eduard Gans, Leopold Zunz, and Moser himself, with the project of modernizing Judaism — making it compatible with the German Enlightenment, putting it on a scientific footing, allowing assimilated German Jews to remain Jews while participating fully in German cultural life. The Society had failed. By 1824 it had effectively dissolved. Several of its members had converted to Lutheranism shortly afterward, including Eduard Gans, the most brilliant of them, who had become a Privatdozent at Berlin in 1825. Gans's conversion had been a kind of opening signal. Heine followed within months.

The letters to Moser, written in the period just after the baptism, contain some of the most acidic self-laceration in nineteenth-century epistolary literature. *I assure you, if the laws had permitted the theft of silver spoons, I would not have allowed myself to be baptized.* The famous line about the certificate as the *Entréebillet zur europäischen Kultur* — the entrance ticket to European culture — comes from the same correspondence. The line is funny, or rather mordant, in the way Heine made his career out of being funny in a register that hurt. What the line conceals, when one reads the letters in sequence, is that Heine never recovered from the certificate. He never quite managed to be either a Jew or a Christian after it. He never forgave himself for the act, and he never undid it.

Daniel has decided that the chapter cannot pretend Heine was undergoing a conversion in the religious sense. The chapter has to be about the ceremony of conversion performed without conversion — the public form filled with no inner content — and about what the emptiness cost the man over the rest of his life.

He opens the manuscript. He writes the date at the top of the page: *28 June 1825.*

{

• • •

}

He had been in Göttingen for nearly two years. The room he kept was on the Burgstrasse, two flights above a bookbinder's shop; the room was small and the rent was reasonable and the window looked across a narrow street to the back wall of the university library. He had expected, when he had arrived in January 1824, to dislike Göttingen. He had disliked it. He had also done his work in it, slowly and unpleasantly and with the sustained dignity of a person who knows that the work is the price of a position.

He was twenty-seven. He was small, slim, dark-haired, with a face that already, at twenty-seven, carried the slight weariness that the lithographs of his middle age would intensify. He had been writing seriously for ten years. He had published two volumes of poetry — the *Gedichte* in 1822, the *Tragödien, nebst einem lyrischen Intermezzo* in 1823 — that had given him a small reputation in literary Berlin and a smaller one elsewhere. He had been corresponding with Goethe. He was the nephew of Salomon Heine, the wealthy Hamburg banker whose monthly stipend kept him in rooms and bread. He had not, in any settled sense, decided what to do with himself.

He had been shaped, more than by anyone else in his childhood, by his mother. Betty Heine — born van Geldern, of an old Düsseldorf medical family — was an educated rationalist of the late Enlightenment, fluent in French, suspicious of pietism, the household member who had read with him, chosen his early tutors, and decided that her son's intelligence was something to be developed rather than constrained. The Jewishness of the household had been observed without conviction. The thinking in the household had been Betty's department, and the thinking had been French and rational and, when religion came up, sceptical. Whatever was Heinean about Heine — the wit, the unsentimental gaze, the resistance to all forms of doctrinal solemnity — had begun with her.

What he had decided, in late winter, was that he would finish his law degree. Why he had decided this was a question he had not entirely settled with himself. The most honest version, when he was honest, was that the law degree was the credential that opened the doors he wanted opened. He wanted, eventually, a position at a university — a chair, a professorship, the kind of academic life that had been theoretically available to a clever young man in the German states in the eighteenth century but that, in the Prussian Cabinet Order of August 18, 1822, had been formally closed to Jews. The Cabinet Order had not invented the exclusion. It had codified what had been the case in practice for a long time. After 1822, however, the matter was settled. A Jew could not hold a professorship in Prussia. The only way to hold a professorship in Prussia was to cease, in the formal sense, to be a Jew.

He had not initially intended to do this. He had been a member of the Verein in Berlin — Gans, Zunz, Moser, the others — and the Verein had been founded on the proposition that the assimilated German Jew could remain a Jew while participating fully in German cultural life. The proposition had been, in retrospect, naive. The Verein had collapsed by 1824. Its members had had to choose. Some had stayed Jewish and accepted the closed doors. Eduard Gans — the brilliant Hegelian legal theorist, the most able of them — had chosen the doors. He had been baptized at the end of 1825, a few months after Heine, although the choice had clearly preceded Heine's. Heine had watched. He had written to Moser — who had stayed Jewish and would stay Jewish — and Moser had written back without judgment. *Do what you must do. I will not love you any less for it.*

This was the morning of the doing. He had risen at six. His bag was packed. He had ordered the carriage for seven. The trip to Heiligenstadt was about twenty-five miles north along the road through the Eichsfeld; with hired horses it would take four hours, perhaps a bit longer if the road was bad. The baptism was scheduled for half past eleven. He intended to be back in Göttingen by evening.

He sat at the small table in his room, dressed already, with a glass of bad coffee in his hand. He looked at the wall opposite, on which hung a framed lithograph of Goethe — bought for him by Moser as a gift two years before — and at the small bookshelf below it. Everything in the room was provisional. He had not put down roots; he had no intention of putting down roots; the law degree was almost finished, and after the degree he intended to go to Hamburg to see his uncle, and after Hamburg he intended to go somewhere — Berlin, perhaps; possibly Paris, he had been wondering whether Paris might be the right place — and the room on the Burgstrasse would be packed up and forgotten.

He had not slept well. He had not slept well in a week. The not-sleeping was not because he had any second thoughts about what he was going to do. He had decided. He was going to do it. The not-sleeping was something else. It was the kind of low-grade, useless interior protest that the body sometimes generates in advance of an action the mind has formally settled and that the body has not been consulted about.

He finished the coffee. He stood. He put on the overcoat that was probably too warm for late June and walked down the two flights of stairs and into the street, where the carriage was already waiting.

{

• • •

}

The road north from Göttingen toward the Eichsfeld passed through villages whose names he had been hearing for two years and whose buildings he had never paid attention to. The countryside was fully in summer. The wheat in the fields was approaching the height a man's hand reached when he stood beside it. The hedgerows were noisy with finches. The morning was warm and getting warmer. He had been right that the overcoat was too much. He removed it after the first hour and folded it on the seat beside him.

He had taken the carriage alone. He had not arranged for any of his Göttingen friends to come with him. The witnesses required for the ceremony would be provided in Heiligenstadt by the pastor, Grimm, with whom he had corresponded twice — a brief exchange of letters arranging the date and the names — and whom he had not yet met. He had not wished for an audience. The point of going to Heiligenstadt rather than to a Göttingen church was the absence of an audience. The Eichsfeld was Catholic, mostly, and Heiligenstadt itself was a Catholic town — a small bishopric, in fact — but there was a Lutheran enclave with a small church, and Pastor Grimm presided over the small Lutheran congregation, and the congregation was small enough that a baptism on a Tuesday in June would attract no notice beyond the parish register.

He thought, on the road, about the names he had selected. He had decided on *Christian Johann Heinrich*. The *Heinrich* was his birth name, the name he had been using as his given name in literary publications since the *Gedichte*. The *Johann* was the standard German Lutheran addition, the John of the gospels. The *Christian* was the name of his entry into Christianity; the name was its own joke; he had written to Moser two months earlier that one might as well wear one's new label visibly on the surface. *Christian* would be the first of the three names. He would not actually use it in his life as it continued; he would continue to publish as *Heinrich Heine*; the *Christian* would be present only in legal documents, where it would do its legal work without ever reaching the literary surface.

He thought also about whether anyone would have understood, if he had attempted to say it aloud, what was wrong with this morning. He concluded, after a few miles, that no one would have. The friends who would have understood — Moser, primarily; perhaps Gans, although Gans had already gone through his own version and had, characteristically, not made a literary subject out of it — were not in the carriage. Goethe in the lithograph above the bookshelf in Göttingen would not have understood, although Goethe might at least have appreciated the irony. The driver on the box outside would not have understood; the driver would have asked who was at fault.

He thought, with some firmness, that he would not allow this morning to acquire the wrong kind of weight. He was going to perform a ceremony. He did not believe in the ceremony. The ceremony would in no way change what he was. He would write a letter to Moser describing the ceremony in terms designed to make Moser laugh, which was his usual way of preventing the things in his life from becoming heavier than they should be permitted to become. He would title the letter, when he wrote it, *Aus Göttingen, nach der Taufe* — From Göttingen, after the baptism. He would write it that evening, or the next day, after he had returned. The letter would contain the line about the silver spoons.

The carriage reached the small wooden bridge over the river outside Witzenhausen. The water below was clear and brown and moving fast. He saw, on the far side, a heron standing in the shallows. The carriage went on.

{

• • •

}

The Lutheran church in Heiligenstadt was small and plain — a converted hall, in fact, that the Lutheran congregation had taken over from a defunct guild in the previous century. The walls were whitewashed. The pews were of unstained pine. A wooden cross hung above a simple pulpit. A baptismal font stood at the front, on the right side, a stone basin on a stone column. There was no organ.

Pastor Gottlob Christian Grimm was waiting at the door. He was a man of perhaps fifty, with a blunt face and the slightly weathered hands of a country pastor who also tended his own garden. He greeted Heine with the careful courtesy of a clergyman who has performed a number of these baptisms over the course of his life and who has long since stopped allowing himself to wonder what was going on inside the candidate. He shook Heine's hand.

He said, in the slightly archaic Lutheran formula: *Friede sei mit Ihnen, Herr Heine.* Peace be with you, Mr. Heine.

Heine returned the formula. He found that he had no difficulty returning it. The formula was a formula. He was here to perform formulas.

Two witnesses had been provided by Grimm. They were a married couple, perhaps in their forties, members of the Lutheran congregation, who had been told that they were standing in for a young law student who was completing his studies and converting prior to taking up a position. Whether they believed the position-prior-to-taking-up part was unclear; they did not look like people who asked many questions. The wife was wearing her good Sunday dress, although it was a Tuesday. She had taken seriously her role as witness.

Grimm led him to the font. The form of the service was the standard Lutheran adult baptism. Grimm asked the questions of the catechism in their canonical order. Heine answered each with the canonical answer. Did he renounce the devil? He renounced the devil. Did he renounce the works of the devil? He renounced the works of the devil. Did he believe in God the Father, maker of heaven and earth? He believed in God the Father, maker of heaven and earth. Did he believe in Jesus Christ his only Son, conceived by the Holy Ghost, born of the Virgin Mary, suffered under Pontius Pilate, was crucified, dead, and buried? He believed in Jesus Christ. The list went on. He answered each line as it came to him with the discipline of a witness in the dock. He did not believe a word of it. Grimm did not, he was quite certain, expect him to believe a word of it. The two witnesses, also, did not particularly care whether he believed any of it. They were here to witness, not to interrogate. The form was the form.

Grimm filled a small ewer with water from the basin. He held it above Heine's head. He asked him to bow. Heine bowed.

The water came down on his head, in three pours, with the trinitarian formula: *Ich taufe dich im Namen des Vaters, und des Sohnes, und des Heiligen Geistes.*

He felt the water. The water was cold. The water was, he found himself thinking, the only physical fact of the ceremony — the only piece of it that registered on the body rather than on the page — and the water was, in itself, indifferent. It had been water before it had touched him; it would be water after; the trinitarian formula did not change the chemistry of the water. He did not know whether this was the correct way to think about a baptism. He did know that it was the way he was thinking about this one.

Grimm spoke the names. *Christian Johann Heinrich Heine.*

The names settled on him. He felt them settle. The first name — *Christian* — was the name of the new identity. He registered it. He did not think of himself as Christian. He would never think of himself as Christian. But the name had been spoken, and the name now existed in the parish register and would exist there forever, and the existence of the name in the register was the thing he had come for. The name was the *Entréebillet*. The name was the document. The name was what the laws of Prussia would, henceforth, find when they searched for him.

Grimm handed him a towel. He dried his hair. He did not look at the witnesses. He did look, briefly, at the cross on the wall above the pulpit. The cross was a plain wooden cross, of dark oak, perhaps a hundred years old. He had nothing to say to the cross. The cross had nothing to say to him. They had been put in the same room by a piece of paperwork, and would be in the same room for another quarter of an hour, and would then never be in the same room again.

Grimm signed the certificate. The witnesses signed. Heine signed. Grimm offered him a small printed copy of the certificate, with the parish seal, which was the actual *Entréebillet*. Heine took it. He folded it in half. He put it in the inside pocket of the overcoat that was folded over his arm. The certificate would, within a few months, be filed with the appropriate Prussian authorities; copies would circulate; the legal status would shift. The room in Heiligenstadt did not need to know any of this. The room had done its part.

Grimm shook his hand again. He said: *God bless you, Christian Johann Heinrich.*

Heine said: *Thank you, Pastor.*

He said it without irony. The irony, he had decided, would be reserved for the letters. The man in the church had done him no harm. The man in the church had performed his part of the formula correctly. The witnesses had not asked the wrong questions. The water had been water. The certificate was in his pocket. He was free to leave.

He left.

{

• • •

}

Outside the church the day had become hot. The Eichsfeld in late June, when the sun was high, was warm in the way that the cold north German interior could occasionally be — a brief and unconvincing summer, with the heat threatening to give way to clouds at any moment. He had several hours before he needed to leave Heiligenstadt; the carriage was waiting at an inn three streets away; the journey back to Göttingen would not begin until at least one o'clock.

He walked. He went away from the church and toward the small market square, which on a Tuesday in late June was modestly busy — a dozen stalls, two of them selling cherries that were the first of the season. He bought a cone of cherries from a woman in a clean white apron. He paid with a small silver coin. He walked back from the square along an unfamiliar street and ate the cherries one at a time, dropping the pits in a small handkerchief he kept folded for this kind of purpose.

He thought, while eating the cherries, about what had just happened. He found that he could not produce, on examination, the indignation he would later perform in the letter to Moser. He had walked into a church, said some words, allowed water to be poured on his head, signed a piece of paper, walked out. The procedure had taken twenty minutes. It had not, in any way he could detect on the inside, transformed him. His Jewishness — whatever that consisted of; he had never been able to give a settled account of what it consisted of, since his upbringing had been observant only in the most attenuated sense and his religion had effectively been a literary one — was unchanged. His not-Christianity was unchanged. He was, exactly as he had been at six o'clock that morning, a small clever man with two slim books of poetry, an unfinished law degree, an uncle in Hamburg, and an interior life that the trinitarian formula had not in the slightest disturbed.

What had changed was a piece of paper. The piece of paper was now in his pocket. The piece of paper was the only thing in the world that was different from the way it had been at six o'clock in the morning.

He turned a corner and found himself in a small lane that ran along the back wall of a Catholic monastery. The monastery's bell was ringing for the noon office. The bell was a small, undignified, slightly cracked bell that had been ringing at noon for several hundred years. He stopped to listen to it. He was, he found, not unhappy. He had imagined that he would be unhappy after the ceremony — that the act would leave a residue of discomfort that would mark the rest of the day. The residue was not there. He was a person walking in an unfamiliar town in early summer with a cone of cherries in his hand. The fact that he had, an hour ago, been baptized was a fact that was now in the parish register and not, particularly, in his body or in his afternoon.

It occurred to him, while standing in the lane and listening to the bell, that the formulation he had been looking for — the one he would write to Moser later that evening — was that the certificate was a kind of *Entréebillet*. An entrance ticket. A ticket of admission. He liked the formulation. He turned it over for a few seconds. *Entréebillet zur europäischen Kultur.* Yes. The ticket of admission to European culture. The phrase had the right register — the casual elevation, the French loanword, the slight self-mockery. He would use it in the letter.

He thought, with a small and entirely unsurprised dryness, that the line he had just composed would probably outlive the work of poetry he was actually trying to make. He had been writing poems for ten years. He had worked carefully on them. He had attended to the meter and the imagery and the structure of the lyric cycle in a way he had attended to almost nothing else in his life. The line about the *Entréebillet* he had composed in twenty seconds, while standing in a lane behind a monastery in Heiligenstadt with cherry pits in a handkerchief in his hand, and the line — he could already see — would survive him. It would survive the *Buch der Lieder*, when he gathered the lyrics into a single volume. It would survive the *Reisebilder*, when he wrote them. It would survive whatever he wrote after that. People in the next century would know the line who would not know any of his actual poems. The line would represent him.

He found this funny rather than tragic. He had, by twenty-seven, accepted that the writer's work was not in any predictable relationship to what would survive. The cherries were ripe. The bell finished ringing. He walked back toward the inn.

{

• • •

}

He returned to Göttingen that evening. He completed his law degree the following month. He never used the law degree. The university position he had baptized himself for did not arrive — partly because his published poetry was already, by 1826, considered too provocative for a professorship; partly because his health declined; partly because he was Heine, and he had been temperamentally unsuited for the academic life he had told himself he wanted. The certificate of baptism that the Prussian authorities accepted as full proof of his civic equality did not, in fact, equalize him in any quarter that had previously found him unequal. The Christian establishment treated him as a Jew. The Jewish community treated him as a renegade. The cynical line about the *Entréebillet* was repeated by both sides as evidence for what each side was claiming.

He moved to Paris in the spring of 1831, after the July Revolution had made France the natural home of liberal German exiles, and lived there for the next twenty-five years. He wrote the *Reisebilder*, the *Romantic School*, the political essays, the poems of the 1840s. He never converted to anything else. He never reconverted to Judaism. He drifted, in the long course of the years, toward what he himself called a personal God of his own — neither the Lutheran God of the Heiligenstadt ceremony nor the God of the synagogue he had been raised on the edge of, but something he assembled from his own reading and his own illness and his own progressive disillusionment with the Hegelian and revolutionary philosophies of his youth.

The illness — almost certainly a form of late syphilis, though some recent scholarship has wondered whether it was multiple sclerosis or some other slow neurological disease — confined him to his bed from 1848 onward. The years on the *Mattratzengruft*, the mattress-grave, the apartment in Paris where he could not move from his pillow, produced some of his greatest work and some of his most surprising statements about belief. He had, in those years, returned to reading the Hebrew Bible. He had identified more strongly with his Jewish heritage than at any time since his Berlin Verein years. He had not, however, undone the certificate. The certificate was in some Prussian archive somewhere. The certificate would outlast him, the way the line about the *Entréebillet* would outlast him.

He died in Paris on February 17, 1856, at the age of fifty-eight. He was buried in Montmartre cemetery, with a Christian funeral that was attended by no priest, because he had asked for no priest. The grave is in the Jewish section of Montmartre by accident — the section not having been formally established at the time of his interment but having grown up around the older graves over the subsequent decades, so that Heine, by the late nineteenth century, was lying among Jewish dead in a Christian cemetery, which is the kind of arrangement his prose would have appreciated.

His reputation in Germany was contested for the rest of the nineteenth century and into the twentieth. He had been a difficult figure for patriotic culture — too political, too cosmopolitan, too Jewish for the Christian establishment, too Christian for the Jewish, too French in his exile, too sharp in his prose. The Nazis, who could not stamp him out because *Die Lorelei* was already a folk song that everyone in Germany knew, attributed the poem to *Verfasser unbekannt* — author unknown — in the school anthologies of the 1930s. After the war the recovery was steady. By the late twentieth century he was firmly canonical in German literature, his place established, the difficulty of fitting him into any tidy national narrative now read as the source of the work's strength rather than as its problem.

He is also, more broadly, one of the great nineteenth-century European lyric poets, particularly for the *Buch der Lieder*, in which the Romantic sentiment of the early stanzas modulates, song by song, into the modern irony and skepticism of the late ones. The transition was Heine's invention. The international reach of his fame is a function of the way the lyric carries across languages and traditions; he is read in French, English, Russian, Spanish; his lines reappear in literatures that owe him directly or indirectly a great deal of the modern lyric's tonal range.

His most durable second life, however, has been in music. The German Lied, which had been a small and largely Schubertian form when Heine began publishing his poetry, found in him a poet of extraordinary suitability for setting — concision, emotional clarity, the volatility of register that gave the composer something to do — and the great song-cycle composers of the nineteenth century returned to him again and again. Schubert set six of the *Buch der Lieder* poems in his last songs of 1828, the *Schwanengesang* group, in the months before his death. Schumann set sixteen in *Dichterliebe* and another nine in the *Liederkreis* op. 24 in 1840, his year of song. Felix Mendelssohn — Heine's contemporary, the next chapter in this book — set *Auf Flügeln des Gesanges* and other lyrics. Brahms returned to him. Hugo Wolf returned to him. Liszt set a number. Richard Strauss returned to him. The German art song repertoire, on any reasonable accounting, is unimaginable without him. The cynic of the *Entréebillet* turned out to be the most musically generative lyric poet of his century.

{

• • •

}

Daniel sets the manuscript aside. Heine has been a different kind of figure to write than Pascal. The Pascal chapter had to find a way to render an experience the writer did not himself believe in. The Heine chapter has had to render the *absence* of an experience — the ceremony performed without inner content — without making the absence into something it was not.

Heine, Daniel thinks, is the figure of the modern conversion. The conversion that is bought rather than given. The conversion the convert himself does not believe in even at the moment he undergoes it. The conversion the laws of the state require and that the inner life refuses to ratify. The figure begins, for the book's purposes, with Heine, and runs through Mendelssohn (born inside an inherited version of the same), and arrives, in the twentieth century, at Schoenberg, who would convert and reconvert and undo what Heine could not bring himself to undo.

What strikes Daniel about Heine — and what makes him difficult to dismiss as a merely cynical figure — is that Heine never made his peace with what he had done. The line about the *Entréebillet* is funny. The line about the silver spoons is funny. Behind both lines, in the letters to Moser and in the late poetry of the *Matratzengruft*, is a man who had bought a freedom he did not enjoy and could not return. Heine was not a hypocrite. Heine was the kind of converter who tells the truth about the conversion as he is performing it, which is in some ways the most morally serious version of the type. He paid for the certificate over thirty years. The payment was the literary work. The literary work, Daniel thinks, is the most honest accounting of a transactional conversion that any literature has produced.

Daniel thinks, as he closes the Heine materials, of how different his own situation has been. He was born in Mexico — a country with a Catholic majority of considerable historical depth, but a country in which the separation of church and state, codified in the constitutional reforms of the nineteenth century, has been taken seriously enough that religion has not been a requisite for full participation in public life. For politicians in Mexico, religious observance has tended to be a weight rather than a credential — public men of his father's and grandfather's generation generally avoided being seen at Mass, on the principle that the office and the pew should not visibly meet. He had inherited that principle without thinking about it. When he had moved to the United States in his twenties, he had found a similar settlement — a constitutional commitment to non-establishment that, in practice, in the cities and states where he had lived, gave the secular citizen the same sense of security and identity that Mexico had.

He had not, in either country, ever been in the position Heine had been in. He had not had to buy a ticket. The countries had not asked him for one. Having a religion, in Mexico and in the United States as he had lived in them, was simply not a requisite — neither a credential that opened any door nor an absence that closed one, neither an advantage nor a disqualification. Whether he had one was a private matter that the public order did not need to know about.

Daniel closes the notebook. He looks at the photograph on the bookshelf to his right. The man in the tallit is, in some Heinrich-Heine sense, a man who had not had the *Entréebillet* available to him; or had had it and refused it; or had not had any need of it because the country and the century in which he had lived had not asked the question. Daniel does not know which. The man in the photograph is silent.

He goes to the listening chair by the north window. He chooses, this evening, the *Buch der Lieder* settings — Schumann's *Dichterliebe* in the recording by Christian Gerhaher and Gerold Huber. The first song begins: *Im wunderschönen Monat Mai, als alle Knospen sprangen.* In the wonderful month of May, when all the buds were bursting open. The poem is from the same lyric cycle as the *Entréebillet* line, written in the same period of Heine's life, and it survives in the German repertoire for reasons that have nothing to do with the certificate in the Prussian archive. He listens.

Figures at the Threshold

Mendelssohn

Daniel sits at the desk. The Mendelssohn materials are out: Eric Werner's older biography (the first to take the Jewish dimension seriously), the more recent R. Larry Todd biography that supplanted it, the letters in the German collected edition, Eduard Devrient's *Erinnerungen* of 1869 in a small Reclam volume, the Bärenreiter score of the *Matthäuspassion*, scores of the *Magnificat*, *Paulus*, the *Lobgesang*, the *Variations sérieuses*, the *Octet*. He has been working on Mendelssohn for two weeks and has not, until now, decided where the chapter's center sits.

Felix Mendelssohn is the only figure in the book who did not himself convert. His father, Abraham Mendelssohn, had the four Mendelssohn children — Fanny, Felix, Rebecka, Paul — baptized as Lutherans in Berlin in 1816, when Felix was seven. Abraham himself was baptized in 1822. The family added the surname *Bartholdy*, borrowed from a brother-in-law who had converted earlier, to mark the new identity. Abraham wrote to Felix in 1829, in a famous letter that is quoted in every account of the family, that there could no more be a Christian Mendelssohn than there could be a Jewish Confucius. Felix accepted the name

Mendelssohn Bartholdy in private correspondence and on official documents. He published his music under *Mendelssohn* alone, or *F. Mendelssohn Bartholdy*, depending on the publication and the audience. He kept the grandfather's name visible. He could not have done otherwise.

The grandfather was the shadow on the inheritance. Moses Mendelssohn — the philosopher of the German-Jewish Enlightenment, the *Phaedon*, the *Jerusalem*, the German translation of the Pentateuch, the friend of Lessing, the figure whom Berlin had called the German Socrates — had died in 1786, twenty-three years before Felix was born. Felix never knew him. He knew the books. The books were on the shelves at the family house in the Leipzigerstrasse. The books were the family's intellectual capital. They were also the residue of the inheritance Abraham had baptized his children out of, and they sat on the shelves because no one in the family was prepared, even in 1816, to take them down.

The chapter is not about a conversion. It is about a young man inhabiting a conversion his father had made for him, with the grandfather's books on the bookshelves, on a single day in March 1829 when he conducted the first public performance of Bach's *Matthäuspassion* since Bach's death seventy-nine years before. The day was Wednesday, March 11. The performance was at the Singakademie in Berlin. Felix was twenty.

The historical event is one of the great moments in nineteenth-century musical history. The chapter has, however, been hard for Daniel to find the angle on, because the event is not about Felix's relationship to his religion. It is about Bach. It is about the Lutheran sacred tradition. It is about the recovery of an enormous work that had been almost lost. Felix's Jewishness — what remained of it, in the second generation — sits in the corner of the chapter, visible to anyone who looks for it, central to no one who does not.

Daniel has decided that the chapter should follow the day, beat by beat, and let the inheritance show itself in the texture rather than in the argument.

He opens the manuscript. He writes the date at the top of the page: *11 March 1829.*

{

• • •

}

He had risen early. The house at Leipzigerstrasse 3 was a deep eighteenth-century town house with a long internal courtyard and a garden behind, set back from one of the great commercial streets of Berlin. The family had been living in it for four years. The garden had a small pavilion at the back, in which the Sunday music meetings — the *Sonntagsmusiken* that had become a fixture of cultivated Berlin — were held in the warm months. In March the pavilion was closed and the family used the music room on the first floor.

Felix had risen at six. The morning was cold. The window of his room looked across the back garden to the corner of the courtyard where the carriage was kept. He washed. He dressed in the dark frock coat his mother had bought him for the previous autumn's concert appearances. He would change before the performance into something a little more formal, but not yet.

He went down to the breakfast room. His sister Fanny was already there, in her dressing gown, reading the previous day's *Vos-*

sische Zeitung with the slight scowl she always had when reading newspapers. Fanny was twenty-three. She was the closest interlocutor on music Felix had ever had — closer than Zelter, closer than any of the visiting older composers he had met in his teens — and she had been the first reader of every score he had written from the *Octet* onward. She would be, in some sense, the first reader of every score he would write, until her death.

She looked up. She said: *Are you ready?*

He said: *I have done what I can do.*

She said: *Sit down. Eat something.*

He sat. The maid brought coffee and rolls. He drank the coffee. He could not eat. Fanny did not press him. She knew his appetite vanished before performances.

Their father came in. Abraham Mendelssohn was forty-three, a successful banker, a serious reader, a more reserved man than his late father had been but with the same Mendelssohnian intelligence in a quieter register. He sat. He said good morning to both of them. He asked, briefly, about the previous evening's rehearsal. Felix answered briefly. Abraham nodded. He did not, on the morning of the performance, want to add to the weight Felix was already carrying. He asked instead about the catering arrangements at the hall, and about whether the King had confirmed his attendance, and about whether there were enough programs. Felix answered each question.

The grandfather's *Phaedon* was on the small bookshelf in the breakfast room — second shelf, fourth volume from the left, with the slightly scorched binding from the time their mother had set the candle too close. Felix looked at it without intending to. The spine was familiar. He had read the *Phaedon* twice — the first time at fifteen because his father had wanted him to, the second time at eighteen because he had found that he wanted to. The book was Moses Mendelssohn's reworking of Plato's *Phaedo*, the dialogue on the immortality of the soul, and it had been one of the most read books in German-speaking Europe in the late eighteenth century. The book was a Jewish Enlightenment text in the form of a Greek philosophical dialogue. The book was, in some sense Felix did not want to investigate too closely on this particular morning, the unspoken text behind everything he was doing this evening.

He drank a second cup of coffee.

What was less visible on the bookshelves but no less present in the household was the connection between his grandfather and the music he was about to conduct. Moses Mendelssohn had been close to the Bach family. He had been a friend of Johann Philipp Kirnberger, one of J. S. Bach's most important students, who had moved to Berlin in the 1750s and lived there until his death in 1783. Kirnberger had been the chief musical theorist at the court of Princess Anna Amalia of Prussia, whose library — eventually subsumed into the Berlin State Library — was one of the great repositories of Bach manuscripts in Europe. Through Kirnberger, and through the Itzig sisters on Felix's mother's side — his great-aunt Sara Levy was a celebrated harpsichordist who had studied with Wilhelm Friedemann Bach and who possessed one of the most important private Bach collections in the city — the Mendelssohn-Itzig circle had become, in the decades after Bach's death in 1750, one of the central nodes of preserved Bach culture in Berlin. The Singakademie itself, where Felix would conduct that evening, had been founded by a Kirnberger pupil,

Carl Friedrich Christian Fasch, and continued under Zelter, Felix's teacher. The line between Bach and Felix went through three generations and four households on both sides of his family. He was not bringing the work back from oblivion. He was bringing it back to a family that had been keeping it alive.

After breakfast he went up to the music room to look one more time at the score. The score was not Bach's autograph — that was in Leipzig, in the Thomasschule library; he had not seen it. The score he had been working from was a manuscript copy made by some hand or other in the eighteenth century, given to him at Christmas 1823 by his grandmother on his mother's side, Bella Salomon. Bella was the maternal grandmother who had not consented to Abraham's conversion of the children and who had remained Jewish to her death. She had nevertheless given her thirteen-year-old grandson, on a Christmas the rest of the family was celebrating in the Christian fashion, the manuscript of the greatest Christian sacred music of the eighteenth century. Bella had said, at the time: *The boy will know what to do with it.* She had not lived to see today; she had died the following year. But she had given him the score.

He had been working on it for nearly six years. He had transcribed his own performance copy with cuts and revisions; he had organized the choruses; he had rehearsed with the Singakademie since the previous autumn. Karl Friedrich Zelter — the Singakademie's director, Felix's teacher, the friend of Goethe — had been doubtful at the start. Zelter had loved Bach his entire life; Zelter had also believed that Bach's music was too complex for any chorus other than a professional one, and the Singakademie was an amateur chorus of merchants and clerks and their wives. Zelter had said, in October, that

Felix's rehearsal sessions were a fine educational exercise but that public performance was not in question. Felix and Devrient had quietly continued. By February Zelter had heard the chorus rehearse the opening double-chorus *Kommt, ihr Töchter, helft mir klagen* and had said only: *Well. Yes. We will see.* He had given his blessing the same afternoon.

The score was on the music stand in the corner. Felix looked at it. He was, he realized, not nervous. He had moved past nervousness several days before. He was in the curious focused calm that descended on him in the hours before any major performance — the same calm he had been in at fourteen when he had conducted the *Midsummer Night's Dream* Overture with a small orchestra, and on a number of occasions since. The state was a kind of disappearance of the personal. The personal — the worry, the consciousness of his age, the consciousness of his name — went away. What remained was the music and the body that was about to move it.

He closed the score. He went back downstairs. His mother Lea had come in from her morning walk. She kissed his forehead. She did not ask whether he was ready. She, like Fanny, did not press him.

He sat in the salon with his mother and Fanny and his younger sister Rebecka and his small brother Paul and his father, in something close to silence, for half an hour. The clock on the mantel ticked. Outside on the Leipzigerstrasse the carriages moved. The hour passed.

{

• • •

}

The Singakademie was a fifteen-minute walk from the Leipzigerstrasse, on the Pariser Platz side of the Unter den Linden, in the building that had been completed for the Akademie in 1827. Felix walked. He preferred to walk before performances. The streets were full at midday — the Berlin merchants, the army of clerks and lawyers and government officials going to their lunch hour — and no one paid particular attention to the small dark young man in the frock coat who walked between them.

Eduard Devrient was at the artists' entrance when he arrived. Devrient was an actor at the Berlin Royal Theater and a singer of considerable accomplishment; he was also Felix's closest male friend; he would be singing the part of Jesus tonight, baritone, the central narrative voice that Bach had written into the role of the suffering Christ. Devrient was thirty, a married man, a generous and warm friend. He greeted Felix with a hand on each shoulder. He said: *Are you eating? You should eat.*

Felix said he had eaten. He had not. Devrient knew this. They went into the hall.

The orchestra was already on the platform tuning. The chorus — about a hundred and fifty singers, the full Singakademie roster augmented for tonight — was in the hall, mostly in the back rows, milling. Devrient took Felix to the conductor's stand. They went over the cuts one more time. Felix had cut nearly a third of Bach's score — recitatives, several arias, some of the choruses he believed the Singakademie could not bring off — and the cuts had been written into Devrient's score and into the orchestral parts. Felix knew them by memory now; he asked Devrient to remind him only of two transitions.

Zelter came up the aisle from the back of the hall. He was sixty-eight, in his Sunday coat, walking with the slight stoop of his last years. He shook Felix's hand. He said: *I was wrong, Felix. I am glad you did not listen to me.*

Felix said: *You let us proceed, Director. That is what mattered.*

Zelter said: *Tonight you will hear what your Bach sounds like in this hall. I was wrong about whether the chorus could do it. I was right that Bach is the greatest of us. We will see.*

Zelter went to his seat in the front row. Felix took the rostrum. He turned to face the chorus and the orchestra. The hall was quiet. He raised his hands.

The afternoon rehearsal was light — only a few passages, only the transitions Felix wanted to confirm, only one full pass through the closing chorus *Wir setzen uns mit Tränen nieder* to make sure the tempo was settled and the chorus had it in the legs. They finished by four. Felix dismissed the chorus and the orchestra at four-fifteen with a short word of thanks. Devrient walked him back to the artists' entrance. They went out and walked the few streets to a small restaurant on the Behrenstrasse where Devrient had his usual table. Devrient ate. Felix sat with him and drank a glass of red wine slowly. They did not speak about the performance. They spoke about Devrient's most recent role at the Royal Theater. The hour passed.

{

• • •

}

He returned to the Singakademie at six. The hall was already half full. He went to the small dressing room at the back, behind the platform, and changed into the formal black coat. He looked at himself in the small mirror. His hair was a little disordered. He combed it. His face was pale. His face was always pale. He found that his hands were steady.

The hall filled. From the dressing room he could hear the murmur grow. He had been told, in the days before, who had said they would attend. The royal family — King Frederick William III and Queen Elisabeth Ludovika — would be in the royal box; the Crown Prince had also confirmed. Hegel — the Hegel, who lectured at the university four streets away and who had been a regular guest at the *Sonntagsmusiken* in the Mendelssohn house — would be in the parquet. Schleiermacher, the great Protestant theologian and preacher, would be in the parquet. The Berlin musical establishment would be in the parquet. The Berlin literary establishment would be in the parquet. His father had said, drily, at breakfast that morning, that there were probably more learned people in the room tonight than in any room in Berlin since the previous April, when there had been a state lecture. Felix had laughed. Abraham had not been entirely joking.

At ten minutes to seven Devrient came to fetch him. They walked together down the small corridor to the platform. The chorus was in place; the orchestra was tuning; the soloists — Anna Milder-Hauptmann, the great Berlin soprano; the bass for the Evangelist; Devrient for Jesus — were assembled to one side. Felix walked to the rostrum. He bowed briefly to the royal box. He turned to the chorus and the orchestra. He raised his hands.

The opening was the great double chorus. *Kommt, ihr Töchter, helft mir klagen.* Come, you daughters, help me lament. The orchestra began with the slow running figure in the strings; the lower voices entered; the upper chorus entered with the boys' chorale *O Lamm Gottes, unschuldig* floating above; the two choruses interwove; the texture filled the hall. Felix conducted with the small precise gestures he had learned from Zelter — the German conducting style of the period, contained, expressive in the wrist rather than in the arm. He had the score on the stand but did not read from it. He had the work in his head.

What he experienced in those first minutes was something he had only experienced before in fragments — in the rehearsal of a passage that suddenly clicked, in certain moments of the *Midsummer Night's Dream* Overture when the pattering staccato in the upper strings had taken on a life of its own. He experienced it now, with the *Matthäuspassion*, in a sustained way that astonished him. The work was conducting itself through him. The work had been conducting itself through itself for a hundred years in manuscript and printed score, with no public performance to release it; the work had been waiting; the work was now finding a public, and the public was, against the odds, the chorus and orchestra he had been training for six months and the seven hundred citizens of Berlin who were sitting silently in the dim hall behind him. The work was in the air.

He moved through the choruses, the chorales, the recitatives, the arias. The chorale *O Haupt voll Blut und Wunden* — Bach's most heartbreaking chorale, which would return five times in the work, each time at a different harmonic and emotional level — happened. The arias of the Evangelist, in their long lyric lines, happened. The chorus *Lass ihn kreuzigen* — let him be crucified — with its terrifying contrapuntal ferocity, happened. Felix was inside the work. He was conducting; he was hearing; he was, in moments, weeping; he did not stop.

The pause between the two parts — Bach had written it as the natural division of the work — Felix observed in the cuts. The chorus and orchestra rested for a few minutes. The hall was silent. Felix did not turn to look at the audience. He did not need to look. He could feel the silence of seven hundred listeners in the way the hall held its air.

The second part began. *Ach, nun ist mein Jesus hin.* The work moved toward the cross. The crowd choruses — *Andern hat er geholfen, Der du den Tempel Gottes zerbrichst* — built and broke and built again. Devrient sang the words from the cross — *Eli, Eli, lama asabthani* — in the simple Aramaic Bach had been faithful to. The chorus closed in on the death. The chorale at the end — *Wenn ich einmal soll scheiden,* when I shall someday depart, the great closing chorale that returns the sufferer's question to the listener — Felix conducted with the chorus seated, almost a whisper, the slowest tempo he had taken anywhere in the work.

Then the closing chorus. *Wir setzen uns mit Tränen nieder.* We sit down with tears. The instrumental closing in the lower strings, descending, ending on the F-sharp minor cadence Bach had written nearly a hundred years before. The hall was silent for a beat after the last chord. Then the applause began.

The applause did not stop for some minutes. Felix turned. He bowed. He turned to the chorus and bowed to the chorus. He turned to the orchestra and bowed to the orchestra. He bowed again. He walked off the platform.

{

• • •

}

He sat in the dressing room for some minutes alone. Devrient came in. Devrient said: *Felix.*

Felix said: *Yes.*

Devrient sat down beside him. He said: *We did it.*

Felix said: *Bach did it. We let him do it.*

Devrient said: *That is also true.*

There were people at the door now — Zelter; the royal chamberlain with a message from the King; the Berlin music critics; some of the chorus. Felix received them. He thanked them. He embraced Zelter for some moments. The chamberlain delivered the King's congratulations and the King's request that the work be performed again, which Felix accepted on behalf of the Singakademie. The critics asked questions, which he answered briefly.

At about ten he and Devrient took a carriage together to go back to the Leipzigerstrasse. Devrient's wife Therese was with them. The carriage moved slowly through the Berlin streets, which were full of people leaving the various theaters and concerts of the evening. The lamps were lit along the Unter den Linden.

In the carriage Felix said, suddenly: *Eduard.*

Devrient said: *Yes?*

Felix said it in the German he and Devrient used between them: *Nun bedenken Sie, dass es ein Komödiant und ein Judenjunge sein mussten, die den Leuten die größte christliche Musik wiederbringen.* Just imagine. That it had to be an actor and a Jew's son to bring back to the people the greatest of Christian music.

He said it in the slightly self-mocking register he used when he was, in fact, dead serious. Devrient laughed. Therese laughed. Felix laughed with them. Devrient would, forty years later, write the line down in his memoir. The line would survive Felix and Devrient and the carriage.

The carriage reached the Leipzigerstrasse. Felix got out. He thanked Devrient and Therese. He went into the house.

Inside, the family was waiting. His father stood up when he came into the salon. Abraham did not say anything at first. He embraced his son. He said, when he stepped back: *Felix. Your grandfather would have been proud of you.* He said it with the slight hesitation of a man who had spent forty years working out his relationship to the grandfather in question and who, on this particular night, had found a formulation that was — for the first time, perhaps — straightforward.

Felix understood which grandfather his father meant. He nodded.

He went up to the music room alone before bed. The score was where he had left it on the stand. He looked at it for a moment. He did not pick it up. He went to the window and looked out across the back garden to the corner of the courtyard where the carriage had been kept that morning. The garden was dark; the small pavilion at the back was dark; the city beyond the garden wall was making the quiet noise it made at night. He stood for a while. He thought of nothing in particular. He thought, briefly and without organizing it into a thought, of the *Phaedon* on the second shelf of the breakfast room.

He went to bed.

{

• • •

}

The eighteen years Felix had left after that night were a sustained productivity of a kind few composers have managed. He continued, all his working life, to compose sacred music in the Bachian and Handelian line he had reaffirmed at the Singakademie. The *Magnificat* in D he had written at thirteen — already, at thirteen, an ambitious choral setting in the Bachian voice, with the *Et misericordia* particularly strong — returned to him in his thinking now that he had inhabited the *Matthäuspassion* from inside. He took elements of its solution, knowingly, into the work to come.

The Bach inheritance was not only programmatic — Felix's revival of the *Matthäuspassion* — but stylistic. His mature compositional language incorporated Bachian contrapuntal technique and choral writing throughout. The fugues in his sacred works, the chorale-cantata architecture of *Paulus* and the cantata sections of the *Lobgesang*, the contrapuntal density of the late string quartets, the six organ sonatas of op. 65 — all carried Bach forward into the nineteenth century in a register no other composer of the Romantic generation managed. Bach's fugal writing and oratorical forms were not, in Felix's hands, historical references. They were the structural ground.

Paulus, the oratorio on Saint Paul, op. 36, premiered at the Lower Rhine Music Festival in Düsseldorf in May 1836, was the first full-scale work of the post-Bach generation in the Bachian-Handelian oratorio form, and it was unmistakably Felix's response to the work he had conducted at twenty. *Paulus* would establish him as the most important sacred composer in Europe. It would be performed across the German-speaking world; it would be sung in English translation in Birmingham, where he would become the central musical figure for the Victorian musical establishment.

He returned to the symphonic-choral form a few years later in the

Lobgesang — the Second Symphony, op. 52, of 1840 — in which three purely orchestral movements give way to a choral cantata in praise of the Word, on Lutheran biblical texts. He returned to the oratorio form one final time in *Elijah*, his last major work, in 1846; that piece is the one for which the broader public eventually remembered him, though it is a work whose extreme popularity has not always served the disciplined scale and concentration of *Paulus*.

He returned to the purely instrumental symphony in two works that, between them, gave the nineteenth century its most successful German evocations of foreign landscape. The *Italian Symphony* — No. 4 in A major, op. 90 — was begun during his Italian travels of 1830 and 1831 and substantially completed by 1833; it is the great Mediterranean light-and-warmth symphony of the German tradition, with the saltarello finale in A minor among the most explicit summonings of place in the symphonic literature. The *Scottish Symphony* — No. 3 in A minor, op. 56 — had begun forming in his head in the summer of 1829, in the ruined chapel of Holyrood Palace in Edinburgh where Mary Queen of Scots had been crowned, and was completed only thirteen years later, in 1842; the slow A-minor introduction of the first movement preserves the cold light of that ruin. Neither symphony is program music in the literal sense. Each succeeds, by purely instrumental means, at carrying a country.

He continued to compose in the other secular forms with the same productivity. The concert overtures begun in his teens — the *Midsummer Night's Dream* of 1826, the *Hebrides* (Fingal's Cave) of 1830, the *Calm Sea and Prosperous Voyage* — became the model for an entire genre in the nineteenth century. The chamber music — the *Octet* he had written at sixteen, the string quintets, the two piano trios in D minor and C minor, the late string quartets — gave the German chamber repertoire some of its most enduring works after the late Beethoven. The piano music, including the *Variations sérieuses* op. 54 of 1841, sat alongside Schumann's solo work as the most serious German pianism of the period; the *Variations sérieuses* themselves were written for a Beethoven memorial album, which is the right context for a set in which the variation form is taken as the tradition's most rigorous test.

He founded the Leipzig Conservatory in 1843. He conducted the Gewandhaus orchestra in Leipzig for the last decade of his life, making it the first orchestra in Europe with a settled, deliberate concert practice — programs designed for the sake of the listener rather than the patron, rehearsals planned for the sake of the music rather than the deadline. The model spread.

He married Cécile Jeanrenaud in 1837. They had five children. He was, by every account, a happy husband and a devoted father. He was also, increasingly, exhausted. The pace he had been keeping since his teens did not slow.

His sister Fanny — also a remarkable composer, who had not been permitted by family or convention to publish under her own name as freely as he had — died in May 1847, of an apoplectic stroke. Felix did not survive her by long. He had a series of strokes himself in October. He died on November 4, 1847, six months after Fanny, at thirty-eight.

{

• • •

}

Daniel sets the manuscript aside. Late evening; past nine. The

Mendelssohn chapter has been the most complex of the four he has written so far, in the way that it has had to do something none of the others required. It has had to render a man not at a threshold but on one side of one — a young composer carrying the inheritance of a turn his father made for him, and using the inheritance to do something specific and beautiful that the world remembered.

Felix Mendelssohn, Daniel thinks, is the figure of the second generation. The first generation of converters — Abraham, the parents of the Heine-and-Mendelssohn cohort — made the decision under the pressures of their period: the post-Napoleonic settlement, the codification of exclusions, the new bourgeois assimilationist project. The first generation had adult selves on the other side of the line. They knew what they had done. Their children — Heine, who at least made the conversion himself in his twenties; Felix, who had had it made for him at seven — knew it differently. Felix never had the option of refusing it. He inherited it the way he inherited the books on the second shelf of the breakfast room.

What strikes Daniel about Felix's inheritance is that he used it well. He did not pretend, the way Heine pretended, that the conversion had not been a conversion. He also did not denounce it. He simply lived in it, and produced — the *Magnificat* at thirteen, the *Octet* at sixteen, the *Midsummer Night's Dream* Overture at seventeen, the *Matthäuspassion* revival at twenty, *Paulus*, the *Lobgesang*, the *Variations sérieuses*, the chamber music, the Leipzig Conservatory, the rebuilt Gewandhaus — work that depended on the inheritance and that, with the inheritance, made his contribution to the German tradition that had baptized him.

The line in the carriage — *ein Komödiant und ein Judenjunge* — is the one moment at which Felix lets the inheritance speak. The line is funny. The line is also serious. The line acknowledges that it is the Jew's son who has restored the greatest of Christian music. The line is the only moment Daniel has been able to find, in the vast Mendelssohn correspondence and in the long records of a public life, where the second-generation position becomes explicit. Everywhere else it is implicit. Felix did not write Heine's letters to Moser. Felix did not need to.

Daniel closes the notebook. He looks at the photograph. The man in the tallit is, if anyone, of Felix's grandfather's generation — perhaps two generations earlier than Felix. The man could have known Moses Mendelssohn. The man could have read the *Phaedon*. Daniel does not know.

He goes to the listening chair by the north window. He chooses, this evening, the *Octet* — the work of the sixteen-year-old Felix, the work that would have been on the music stand at the Leipzigerstrasse on the morning of March 11, 1829, alongside the *Matthäuspassion* score. The first movement begins: an ascending E-flat major arpeggio in the first violin, the sixteen-year-old Felix announcing that he had already arrived.

Figures at the Threshold

Newman

Daniel sits at the desk. The Newman materials are out: the *Apologia Pro Vita Sua* in the Penguin edition; the *Essay on the Development of Christian Doctrine*; the *Letters and Diaries*; the *Parochial and Plain Sermons*; the Ker biography; *Tracts for the Times*; the small volume containing *Lead, Kindly Light* and *The Dream of Gerontius*.

Newman is the most exhaustively documented religious conversion in the English-language tradition. The *Apologia* — written in seven weeks during the spring of 1864, in response to Charles Kingsley's accusation that Newman had not held the truth as a virtue — became one of the great spiritual autobiographies in English and settled the question publicly. Daniel has been reading it for the third time in his life.

What he finds difficult about the chapter is what is also true: the conversion is so thoroughly self-narrated that any account works in the shadow of the *Apologia*'s own settled telling. The angle Daniel has chosen is the one the *Apologia* itself does not quite take — the day, October 9, 1845, at Littlemore, the day the form caught up with the long substance.

Newman was forty-four. He had been an Anglican priest for twenty years and the most famous Anglican of his generation since the early 1830s, when the Oxford Movement had begun. Tract 90 of 1841, in which he had argued that the Thirty-Nine Articles could be read in a Catholic sense, had ended his Anglican career. He had resigned the parish of Saint Mary the Virgin in September 1843 and withdrawn from his Oriel fellowship in early 1845. He had spent the years since 1842 at Littlemore, in a row of converted cottages with a small community of young men who had been moving with him toward the same conclusion. By the autumn of 1845 the conclusion was complete. The *Essay on Development*, which he had been writing through the spring and summer, was the intellectual case. The case was finished. The reception by Father Dominic Barberi, when it came on October 9, was the form catching up with the substance.

He opens the manuscript. He writes the date: *9 October 1845.*

{

• • •

}

The cottages at Littlemore stood in a row along a country lane south of the village. They had been a small school until 1839, when Newman had bought them and converted them into a household — a set of bedrooms, a chapel, a refectory, no canonical status in the Church of England, no continental Catholic precedent, the kind of thing that comes into being when serious religious men in their forties decide they have nowhere else to go.

The afternoon of October 8 was overcast and cold, with a steady rain since lunchtime. Newman had spent the morning over the proofs of the *Essay on Development* and after lunch had walked to the village post office to send a letter to his only living sister, Jemima Mozley, who would not approve of what was about to happen. By three he was back in his room. The room was simple — a bed, a chair, a writing-table, a small bookshelf, a crucifix on the wall. He had been in this room for three years. The room had become the room in which the question that had been with him since 1839 had been worked through.

What had been hardest in the last months was not the intellectual case. The case was settled. What had been hardest was the parish work he was leaving — the men he had married, the children he had baptized, the dying he had attended. He was about to stop being a parish priest. He was about to become a Catholic in England in 1845, which was a marginal and slightly exotic thing to be. He thought also of the friends. Edward Pusey would not convert; Pusey would nevertheless remain his friend until Pusey's death in 1882. John Keble would not convert; that relationship would be more painful. Hurrell Froude, the third of the original Tractarian intimates, was nine years dead of consumption. Newman thought of him this afternoon, briefly, at the window. Froude had not had to choose.

He went down to the small refectory at four. Three of the household were there — John Dalgairns, William Lockhart, and Ambrose St. John, all already received themselves earlier in 1845, all waiting for him to follow. He drank a cup of tea. He blessed the small group, in the Anglican formula he would never use again. The formula tonight was still his to give. He went back upstairs and waited.

{

• • •

}

Father Dominic Barberi arrived at half past nine, with two companion priests. The rain had held grim from Aston onward; the three of them came up to the door in a small puddle of rainwater, with their black cloaks streaming.

Barberi was fifty-three, small, round-faced, dark-eyed, the warm Italian look that did not match his English surroundings. His English was poor and accented. He had been in England for four years as a Passionist missionary, founding the Aston Hall mission in Staffordshire, walking across English fields in his cassock under astonished eyes, refused service at inns, pelted with stones in the streets. He had taken all of it as part of the missionary task. He was a peasant's son from the Papal States in whom his superiors had recognized a quality of patient endurance that the work would require.

Newman led him into the small parlor where a fire had been kept. He gave Barberi his own dry coat. The two younger Passionists were taken upstairs to dry off.

Newman and Barberi sat by the fire. There was a small silence. Then Barberi said, in his careful broken English: *Mr. Newman. I am ready when you are ready.*

Newman said: *I am ready, Father.*

He stood up. He walked the few steps to where Barberi was sitting. He knelt. He said, in the formula he had prepared: *I beg leave to be received into the Catholic Church.*

Barberi looked at him. He blessed him. He said, in Italian, half to himself: *Sia benedetto il nome del Signore.* Blessed be the name of the Lord.

{

• • •

}

Barberi said: *We must hear your confession. The general confession, of all your life. Tonight, then tomorrow morning the reception, the conditional baptism for the safety, the first Mass.*

They knelt together by the fire. Barberi produced his stole, which had survived the rain folded in oilcloth. He put it around his neck.

Newman spoke for nearly two hours. He had been preparing — not in writing, but in the slow internal review of his life — for months. He spoke of the small sins of childhood, the early Evangelical arrogance at sixteen, the impatience of the Oxford Movement years with men who could not see what he was beginning to see, his treatment of his mother in her last illness, the friendship with Hurrell Froude, the long friendship with Keble he was about to wound. He spoke of his pride, which had been his organizing weakness throughout his life. He spoke of the years between 1839, when the question of Rome had first opened seriously in him, and the present evening, with their many equivocations.

Barberi listened in his careful way. He said, in his fragmented but unmistakable English: *Mr. Newman. The Lord has been very patient with you. The Lord is patient with all of us. Tomorrow you come into His Church.* He gave the absolution.

Newman rose. He felt, for the first time in many weeks, light in the body. He had been carrying the weight of the whole life, and the weight was, for the duration of that absolution, set down.

Barberi said: *Now you must sleep.*

{

• • •

}

He did not sleep well. He rose at five. The morning was cold and clear; the rain had stopped. He prayed his Anglican Morning Prayer for the last time, the small Prayer Book in his hand the one his mother had given him long before. He read the Psalms. He closed the book. He went down to the chapel.

The chapel was small — the school's old main classroom, adapted with an altar at the east end, a wooden communion rail, plain pews, whitewashed walls, a single small crucifix. Today it would, for the first time, be used for a Catholic Mass.

Frederick Bowles and Richard Stanton would be received with him; Ambrose St. John would assist. Barberi was already in the chapel, in his Passionist habit, with the alb and stole and chasuble. The altar had been prepared the previous evening — candles, linen, the small chalice one of Barberi's Birmingham congregation had sent down with him.

Newman knelt in the front pew. Barberi began.

The conditional baptism was first. The Catholic Church accepted Anglican baptism as ordinarily valid; the conditional rite was a precaution. Barberi spoke the formula in Latin: *Si non es baptizatus, ego te baptizo in nomine Patris et Filii et Spiritus Sancti.* The water came down on Newman's forehead.

The Mass began. The Latin was the Latin Newman had been reading in the breviary and the missal for years; he had been praying the Roman Office privately in Latin since 1842, in a kind of advance preparation. The Latin was, on this morning, the language he had been moving toward all his life.

The familiar parts arrived in their order: Introit, Kyrie, Gloria, Collect, Epistle, Gospel, Credo. *Credo in unum Deum, Patrem omnipotentem, factorem caeli et terrae.* The Offertory. The Sanctus. The Canon, prayed in the silent voice of the Latin rite, with only the small lifting of Barberi's hands at the consecration visible.

The consecration came. Barberi held up the host. The bell rang.

Newman bowed his head. He had read more about the Eucharist than almost any English Protestant of his century. He had written about it. He had defended it in the *Tracts*. He had never received it as a Catholic. The receiving was the moment everything had been pointing toward.

When the time for communion came, he approached the altar rail. He knelt. Barberi placed the host on his tongue. *Corpus Domini nostri Iesu Christi custodiat animam tuam in vitam aeternam. Amen.*

Newman closed his eyes. He held the host in his mouth without swallowing. He opened his eyes. He swallowed. He stood. He walked back to his pew. He knelt. He put his face in his hands.

He had crossed.

{

• • •

}

The Mass ended. Barberi blessed Bowles and Stanton, embraced Newman, took breakfast in the small refectory, and left for the carriage to Banbury by eleven. He blessed Newman one more time at the door. He said: *Mr. Newman. I will pray for you every day.* Newman said: *Father, I will pray for you every day.* The carriage moved off down the lane.

The rest of the day continued on the principle that nothing had happened. Newman wrote brief notes to Pusey and Keble. He walked alone along the lane south from the cottages, past the field where he had walked many times in the previous three years, into the next field, and back. He came back at four. He opened the breviary and read the Office of the day in the new register.

{

• • •

}

The years that followed were settled by the act of October 9. He resigned his Oriel fellowship within weeks. He left Littlemore in February 1846, went to Rome, and was ordained a Catholic priest by the Cardinal of Propaganda Fide on May 30, 1847. He returned to England as a member of the Congregation of the Oratory of Saint Philip Neri. The Oratory at Birmingham, which he established at Edgbaston, would be his home for the next forty-three years.

The English Catholic establishment received him with mixed feelings. He clashed with Cardinal Wiseman and, more painfully, with Henry Edward Manning. The Catholic University of Ireland he founded in 1854 did not flourish; the *Idea of a University* lectures he gave for it survived as the great English-language statement on liberal education.

The *Apologia Pro Vita Sua* of 1864 settled the question publicly. In 1879 Pope Leo XIII made him a Cardinal. He took as his motto *Cor ad cor loquitur* — heart speaks to heart. He died at the Birmingham Oratory on August 11, 1890, at eighty-nine. He was buried, at his own request, in the same grave as his closest friend Ambrose St. John, who had died in 1875. He was beatified in 2010 and canonized by Pope Francis in 2019.

{

• • •

}

Daniel sets the manuscript aside. The Newman chapter has been a different formal challenge from the previous ones. Pascal's was the rendering of a sudden experience. Heine's, the rendering of an empty ceremony. Mendelssohn's, the rendering of an inhabited inheritance. Newman's has been the rendering of a slow, intellectually sustained, humanly costly conversion that arrived at its formal moment after years of work.

What is also visible in the chapter, and worth marking, is the texture of nineteenth-century Christian-on-Christian recruitment. Father Dominic Barberi was a Passionist — Daniel had to look the Passionists up, who turn out to be one of the smaller modern Catholic orders, founded in 1720 by Saint Paul of the Cross, distinct from the Dominicans (the thirteenth-century Order of Preachers), the Jesuits, the Benedictines, and the Oratorians of Saint Philip Neri whom Newman would eventually join. The English Catholic mission of the 1840s was a scrappy, multi-order affair, and the distinctions among the orders had not been Daniel's department before he sat down to write. Barberi had walked across English fields in his black cassock under astonished eyes, had been pelted with stones in the streets, had been refused service at inns; he had taken all of it as part of the missionary task. Compared with what European Christianity had been capable of in the religious wars of the sixteenth and seventeenth centuries — the Saint Bartholomew's Day massacre, the Thirty Years' War, the long cycles of Protestant and Catholic killing — the treatment of Barberi was mild. Compared with the secular tolerance of the country Daniel grew up in, it was the surviving residue of a longer and harsher pattern. The thread will continue, in this book, through the Greene and Waugh chapters: the small English Catholic minority of the twentieth century was the intellectual heir of the small audience that had received Barberi.

What also strikes Daniel, on rereading, is the formula Barberi used at the end of the confession: *The Lord has been very patient with you.* Spoken by an Italian Passionist with broken English, in a small parlor in a Berkshire village, by a fire, to a man who had been Vicar of Saint Mary the Virgin for fifteen years. The formula speaks for God. The priest stands in for the divine patience. Daniel, the twenty-first-century lawyer, finds this striking — the assumption that the priest is authorized to ventriloquize the Lord's disposition. He does not contest it within the frame of the chapter; the formula is what Barberi said, and Newman accepted it, and the chapter records it. He does, however, register it as a piece of nineteenth-century Catholic practice that the twenty-first century has largely lost the ear for.

What strikes Daniel about Newman, once these things are noted, is the clarity. The conversion was not given to him in the form of fire; it was not bought; it was not inherited. It was earned, in a sense the lawyer in Daniel is forced to recognize as legitimate. Newman had read the Fathers; he had worked through the question of doctrinal development; he had taken his time; he had allowed each piece of the argument to settle before moving to the next; and at the end the conclusion had been there, waiting.

But Daniel, the cynic and student of human nature, has his small reservations. The work was honest. The conclusion followed. The conclusion also took Newman, eventually, to the Cardinal's hat in 1879 and to a position of major Catholic eminence that he would never have achieved as an Anglican. Daniel does not assert that the eventual eminence was a motive — Newman's correspondence does not support that claim, and the *Apologia* does not, and Newman's own decades of being passed over by the English Catholic hierarchy under Wiseman and Manning do not. Daniel does, however, register that fame and position are forms human nature takes wherever it arrives, and that the lawyer in him cannot, when he looks at any major conversion that ends in eminence, entirely set the question aside. He notes it without insisting on it.

What this means for the book, Daniel thinks, is that the religious conversion is not a single phenomenon. It is a category that contains the experience and the bargain and the inheritance and the argument and, sometimes, the position acquired through conversion, and the five are not finally reducible to one another. Newman is the limit case for the argument type. The honesty of the work does not dissolve every shadow Daniel can see in it; nor does the shadow dissolve the honesty.

Daniel closes the notebook. He looks at the photograph. He goes to the listening chair. He chooses, this evening, the *Dream of Gerontius* — the Edward Elgar oratorio of 1900, on Newman's poem of 1865 about the soul of a dying man being escorted by his guardian angel to judgment. The recording is the Barbirolli with the Hallé Orchestra and Janet Baker, which Daniel has been listening to for fifty years. The dying man begins to speak: *Jesu, Maria — I am near to death, and Thou art calling me; I know it now.*

Figures at the Threshold

Huysmans

Daniel sits at the desk. The Huysmans materials are out: the Pléiade edition of *À rebours* and *Là-bas; En route* in the Folio Classique; *La Cathédrale; L'Oblat*; the *Lettres* in the Cerf volume; the Robert Baldick biography in English; the Pierre Cogny critical study in French. He has been working on Huysmans for two weeks.

Huysmans is the aesthete's turn. He represents — in the lineage of religious conversion in the modern period — a specific type that the previous chapters do not contain. He did not convert through argument, as Newman did; he did not convert through a sudden interior fire, as Pascal did; he did not buy his conversion, as Heine did; he did not inherit one, as Mendelssohn had it inherited for him. He converted through art. He converted because the art he had been pursuing for twenty years — the *Naturalism* of his apprenticeship in Zola's circle, the *decadence* of *À rebours* and *Là-bas* — had brought him, slowly and against his earlier intentions, to the door of the Catholic Church.

What he found at the door was beauty. That was the only thing it had been possible for him to find. He was not looking for argument; the argument did not interest him. He was not looking for moral consolation; he was a Parisian who had stopped expecting moral consolation from any institution. He was looking, although he had not at first known he was looking, for the specific kind of beauty that a serious religious tradition produces and that no other human enterprise can produce — the Gregorian chant of the offices, the Romanesque and Gothic architecture of the great churches, the iconography of the saints, the liturgical year as a kind of spiritual architecture. He had been writing about all of this in the late 1880s and early 1890s without yet having taken the step of submitting himself to it. In July of 1892 he took the step.

The step was a week at La Trappe de Notre-Dame d'Igny, a Cistercian monastery in the Aube, about a hundred and twenty kilometers east of Paris. He had been advised to go there by his confessor, the Abbé Arthur Mugnier of Sainte-Clotilde, the famous Parisian priest who heard the confessions of half the literary establishment of the Belle Époque. Mugnier had told him that the slow movement of his last several years would not complete itself in Paris. He needed silence. He needed the rule of an order. Huysmans had agreed. He had taken a week of leave from his position at the Ministry of the Interior, where he had been a civil servant for twenty-six years, and he had taken the train east.

He was forty-four. He was the author of the bible of aesthetic decadence. He was about to make his first confession in twenty-five years.

Daniel writes the date at the top of the page: *July 1892.*

{

• • •

}

He arrived at Igny on the afternoon of Tuesday, July 12, by the carriage that ran twice a week from the small station at Fismes. The drive had taken three hours over country roads that had not been improved in the previous decade. The summer was at its height. The wheat in the fields had been cut. The cicadas were loud. The monastery was a cluster of pale stone buildings set back from the road, with a small belltower and a long, low gatehouse.

The brother porter — an old man, in the Cistercian white robe with the black scapular — opened the small door in the gate and looked at him with the careful neutrality that the porter of a Trappist monastery has cultivated as the appropriate response to all arrivals. Huysmans gave his name. The porter checked the small book on the shelf inside the gatehouse. The name was there, with the dates of his stay. The porter showed him in.

The inner courtyard was quiet. Huysmans had expected this; he had read enough about Cistercian houses to know that silence was the first rule. What he had not expected was the specific weight of the silence — the way it seemed to come up from the stones, to be older than the porter, to be older than the buildings, to be in some sense the building's actual material.

The porter led him to the *hôtellerie* — the guest quarters — and showed him to a small whitewashed cell with a narrow bed, a wooden table, a chair, a crucifix on the wall, and a single window that looked out on the kitchen garden. *Vespers at five thirty,* the porter said. *Supper at six. Compline at seven thirty.*

Huysmans sat on the bed. He had brought one bag: a change of linen, a missal, a copy of the *Imitation of Christ*, his breviary. He had not brought the cigarettes he had been smoking for twenty-five years; the rules of the *hôtellerie* did not permit them. He had not brought the Parisian newspapers. He had not brought writing paper. He had brought himself.

{

• • •

}

The *père hôtelier* came for him at five — a tall thin monk of perhaps fifty, also in the white and black, with a face that had been weathered by the open work in the kitchen garden. He led Huysmans through the cloister to the church.

The church at Igny was simple, in the Cistercian style — austere, unornamented, with a clean stone interior and high vaults. The choir was at the far end, behind a small wooden grille. The brothers were already entering by a side door. Huysmans was led to the visitors' bench at the back of the nave. He sat. He waited.

The bell rang. The brothers stood. The cantor intoned the opening of the office: *Deus, in adiutorium meum intende.*

The choir responded: *Domine, ad adiuvandum me festina.*

The Gregorian chant came up out of the choir in the way that Gregorian chant comes up — the unison line, the slow modal phrases, the absence of harmony, the absence of any of the apparatus of polyphony or instrumental accompaniment that would later accumulate around Christian sacred music in the centuries after the Cistercians. Huysmans had been listening to chant at Notre-Dame and Saint-Sulpice for several years. He had written about it in his journalism. He had not, however, until this moment, heard chant as it was meant to be heard, which was sung by men who lived inside it, in a building built for it, in the hour of the office for which it had been composed, with no one in the church other than the choir and the small group of guests who were there to overhear.

He sat without moving. The Vespers psalms went by — Psalm 109, Psalm 110, Psalm 111. The little chapter. The hymn. The *Magnificat*. The collect. The brothers filed out. The church returned to its silence.

Huysmans did not stand up immediately. He did not weep. He did not, he thought afterward, have any particular interior experience of the kind he had been told to expect. He had simply heard a thing that he had been writing about for several years and that he had not, until that moment, understood. The understanding was not an argument. The understanding was that the music he had been describing in the *feuilletons* and the novels — the medieval depth, the Cistercian severity, the chant as the spine of the Catholic interior — was an actual thing that actual men actually sang in actual churches, and that the actual thing was, in person, more than what he had been able to put on the page. He had written approximately. The actual was not approximate.

{

• • •

}

On the morning of Thursday, July 14 — the day, in Paris, of the Bastille fireworks and the Republic's annual celebration of itself — he made his confession.

The *père hôtelier* had arranged it with the prior. The prior was Dom Augustin Marre, a man of sixty, firm, intelligent, patient, who would later become abbot of Igny and eventually of Sept-Fons. He met Huysmans in a small room off the cloister that was used for these encounters.

Huysmans knelt. He had been preparing, in the quiet of his cell over the previous days, the catalogue of what he had to confess. The catalogue went back, in earnest, twenty-five years. He had not been to confession since he was eighteen.

He spoke. He spoke of his Parisian life — the women, the small immoralities, the appetites that had organized themselves into habits over a quarter of a century. He spoke of the books. He spoke of *À rebours* — the bible of aesthetic decadence, the book that had given Des Esseintes to the world, the book the Catholic establishment had read with the specific concern that turned, sometimes, into something more, and that had brought Huysmans to the attention of confessors he had not yet met. He spoke of *Là-bas* — the satanism research, the dark medieval, Gilles de Rais, the long evenings he had spent in the company of bad men in the Parisian fringe to gather the material. He spoke of his pride. He spoke of what he had failed to do for the people in his life who had needed him, including his mother.

Dom Augustin listened without interrupting. When Huysmans had finished, the prior was silent for some moments. Then he said: *Monsieur Huysmans. The Lord has been calling you for a long time. You have been listening to the call without answering it. The time has come to answer.* He gave the absolution.

Huysmans rose. He found that he could not, for some seconds, see properly. The room was a little dim and the small window let in the grey light of an Aube morning that was preparing to be hot. He blinked. He sat in the chair across from the prior. The prior smiled. He said: *You will receive communion tomorrow morning.*

Huysmans said: *Thank you, Father.*

{

• • •

}

He did not sleep that night. He attended Vigils. He attended Lauds. He attended Prime. The Mass was at seven. He had not received communion in twenty-five years.

He approached the altar rail with the small group of visitors who were there for the same reason — half a dozen lay men, mostly older than he was, who had been making retreats. He knelt. The celebrant placed the host on his tongue. The Latin formula came: *Corpus Domini nostri Iesu Christi custodiat animam tuam in vitam aeternam.*

Huysmans closed his eyes. He held the host on his tongue without immediately swallowing it. He felt, in the way one feels in moments of acute attention, the particular dryness of the wafer, the smallness of it, the way it dissolved slightly against the tongue. He did not feel ecstasy. He did not feel, on examination, any of the specific emotions that converts have reported as the marker of the moment. What he felt was that he had returned. He had not been returning to a place he had ever been; he had been baptized as an infant, he had made his first communion as a child, he had not lived inside the Catholic Church as an adult. What he was returning to, when he tried to describe the feeling to himself afterward, was not the country but the question of the country. He had spent twenty-five years organizing his life around the assumption that the country did not exist. He was, on the morning of Friday, July 15, 1892, in the church at Igny, taking the host of a place whose existence he had been denying. The host did not argue with him. The host let him have the moment.

He swallowed. He stood. He returned to the bench. He knelt with his face in his hands for some minutes. The Mass continued.

{

• • •

}

He left Igny on Tuesday, July 19. The carriage took him back to Fismes, and the train back to Paris. He returned to his apartment. He returned to his desk at the Ministry of the Interior on Wednesday morning. The civil-service work was unchanged.

What had changed was everything around the work. He had begun, on the train back from Fismes, to take notes for a novel. The novel would become *En route*, published in 1895, the first volume of what he would later call the *Durtal* trilogy — Durtal being the autobiographical figure who had appeared in *Là-bas* and who would now follow Huysmans through *La Cathédrale* (1898) and *L'Oblat* (1903). *En route* fictionalized the Igny week with very little disguise. The book sold. It was attacked — by the secular literary establishment for sentimentality, by the Catholic establishment for insufficient orthodoxy. Huysmans did not particularly mind the attacks. The book had said what he wanted said.

Over the next decade his life slowly conformed to the shape the Igny week had given it. In 1899 he made his oblation as a Benedictine oblate at the Abbey of Saint-Martin de Ligugé. The oblation made him a member of the Benedictine family without binding him to monastic vows; he remained in the world, with a rule of life, and could attend the offices when he was at Ligugé. He spent considerable time there. *L'Oblat* (1903) is the novel of this last phase.

His relationship to the books that had brought him to the door — *À rebours* and *Là-bas*, the books the Catholic establishment had read with concern and that he himself, after Igny, came to think of as a stage rather than a destination — was complex. He did not ask his publisher to stop printing them. He did not suppress them. He did not formally repudiate them. In 1903 he wrote a long preface to *À rebours*, twenty years after the original publication, in which he addressed the book retrospectively, acknowledged the path that had led from it to the church, and described it as the work of a man at one stage of an itinerary that had since continued. He let the books stand. They had been part of how he had arrived where he eventually arrived.

His later writing developed a polemical edge. He was not, in the manner of certain Catholic apologists, principally against atheists or agnostics; his attacks were directed instead at the secularized worldly Catholicism of late-nineteenth-century French society, at the liberal Catholicism that he believed had emptied the doctrinal core, at the occultism he had researched too closely for *Là-bas* and had come to regard as a real and dangerous thing, and at the religious indifference of the educated classes. He had become, in his last decade, a militant — not in the sense of evangelizing the unconverted but in the sense of policing the converted.

He died in Paris on May 12, 1907, at fifty-nine, of cancer of the jaw. He had refused morphine in the last weeks; he had wished to suffer the death consciously, as a discipline. He had been received into the Carmelite Third Order in his final illness. He was buried at the Cimetière de Montparnasse.

{

• • •

}

Daniel sets the manuscript aside. The Huysmans chapter has moved him in a way the previous chapters have not. With Spinoza he had read with the lawyer's fellowship for another man's brief; with Pascal with the lawyer's distance from a witness whose testimony he could not adjudicate; with Heine with the recognition of a familiar cynicism; with Mendelssohn with the historian's appreciation of a complex inheritance; with Newman with respect for the work and a small reservation about the eminence. With Huysmans he has read with commonality. The mystery of the sacred music — the Bach Passions, the Mendelssohn *Magnificat*, the Gregorian chant — has been Daniel's mystery as well, in his listening chair for fifty years. The Romanesque churches, the Cistercian abbeys, the figure of the seated stone Christ on a French capital — these have been Daniel's territory. Huysmans had come into the church through the door Daniel had been standing at without crossing, honestly convinced that he will not cross it.

The Huysmans chapter has been, in this sense, the chapter of beauty as the route to the threshold. Pascal had the fire; Spinoza had the geometry; Newman had the Fathers and the development of doctrine; Heine had the Prussian Cabinet Order; Mendelssohn had the inheritance; Huysmans had the Gregorian chant and the Romanesque and the long accumulating glamour of the Catholic interior. Huysmans had what Daniel himself has been spending fifty years touching without quite touching. It is not in Daniel's nature to cross. It is not his ideology. The spirituality he enjoys is internal — his own — without the need of a dogma; he is convinced that this life is final, and he is happy with that conclusion. The Romanesque of Castile. The

Cistercian abbeys. La Tourette and Ronchamp. Bach, Handel, Mendelssohn, Brahms, Fauré, Duruflé. The whole apparatus of European sacred art, which Daniel has been listening to and reading and traveling to see for most of his adult life, is the apparatus that brought Huysmans to the door of the church.

The difference, Daniel thinks, is the temperament. Huysmans was the kind of man who, when he stood in the Cistercian church at Igny and heard the chant for the first time as it was meant to be heard, knew that he had been moving toward this room for years and was now in it. Daniel is the kind of man who, when he stands in a Cistercian church and hears chant, registers the beauty with attention and respect, walks out, goes to the next church on the itinerary, and the beauty does not become a question about his own life. The aesthetic, in Huysmans, was a route. The aesthetic, in Daniel, has been a destination.

The further difference is what Huysmans accepted at the end of the route — the strict rule, the daily submission to its discipline, the membership of its community, the participation in its rite. The Huysmans of the late work, militant in his Catholicism, was the figure who had gone all the way through the door and was now engaged in the long internal work of policing what was on the other side. Daniel, if pressed to name his own theological position, would describe himself as a kind of Spinozist — not in the technical sense of the *Ethics*, but in the looser sense of a man who recognizes the world as a single substance within which he is a small modification, who finds the major institutional religions historically and morally interesting but personally unnecessary, who does not require a community to mediate between himself and what is, who does not require a rite to order what would otherwise be unordered. Huysmans needed the rule. Daniel does not.

This is, Daniel acknowledges, a difference that may run deeper than temperament. Huysmans had a metaphysical hunger that the beauty awakened. Daniel does not, as far as he can tell, have that hunger; or, if he has it, the hunger has been satisfied — if that is the word — by the secular intellectual life he has built and that has, on the evidence of seventy-eight years, been sufficient. The beauty has been the thing itself, not the door to a further thing.

And yet — Daniel acknowledges, in fairness — there has been one night that resembled what Huysmans found in the chant at Igny. Sixty years ago, in his early twenties, traveling in France with an architect friend whose mentor had given him a letter of introduction to the prior of La Tourette — the Dominican convent near Lyon designed by Le Corbusier — he and his friend had been received as guests for one night. They were given two of the long row of monks' cells along the upper level: narrow, a single bed, a small bathroom, a wooden desk of the simplest construction, a chair, a crucifix — the same bare furniture Huysmans had found at Igny seventy years before. The one difference was the small terrace at the end of each cell, which Le Corbusier had designed for them, looking out across the forest below the convent.

The forest was in autumn. The night was cold. After the simple meal in the refectory below, eaten with the brothers in silence, Daniel had gone back to his cell and out onto the terrace and stood there for an hour. The sky was clear. The stars were as bright as he had ever seen them. The cold and the silence and the stars produced in him a state he could not, in the years since, name with any precision. The closest available term was *almost-religious.* He was twenty-three. He stood there until his hands were too cold, then he closed the door.

The next morning he and his friend — his friend was Jewish; they had both been received by the Dominicans with the same simple courtesy — attended the Mass in the chapel Le Corbusier had built. They were not Catholics. They were not asked to do anything they were not prepared to do. They sat at the back. The light through the strange small slits and colored panels moved across the concrete walls in the way the architect had specified. The Mass ended. They left.

That was sixty years ago. Daniel still remembers it. The remembering is a fact of his interior life that has not weakened with the decades. But it did not become a route. It became a memory. It is on the terrace at La Tourette, not at the altar at Igny, that Daniel still stands.

He closes the notebook. He goes to the listening chair. He chooses, this evening, a recording of Gregorian chant by the Choir of the Monks of the Abbey of Saint-Pierre de Solesmes — the standard recording of the late twentieth century, in the *Vespers and Compline* selection, the office for the season of Pentecost. The opening of Vespers begins: *Deus, in adiutorium meum intende.*

Figures at the Threshold

Claudel

Daniel sits at the desk. The Claudel materials are out: the *Œuvres complètes* in the Pléiade; *Cinq Grandes Odes; L'Annonce faite à Marie; Le Soulier de satin; Partage de Midi*; the *Mémoires improvisés* — Claudel's late spoken autobiography, given on French radio in 1951; the small Pléiade essay *Ma conversion* of 1913, in which Claudel set down the canonical account of the moment in Notre-Dame; the biographies by Henri Guillemin and Gérald Antoine; the *Correspondance avec André Gide* in the Folio Classique. He has been working on Claudel for two weeks.

Claudel is the chapter of the instantaneous conversion. He represents — alongside Pascal — the type in which the decisive moment is short. Pascal's was two hours. Claudel's was, by his own testimony, an instant. *En un instant mon cœur fut touché et je crus.* In an instant my heart was touched and I believed. He wrote the line in 1913, twenty-seven years after the moment in question; the moment had organized the rest of his life, and the formulation he gave to it had been worked out across the decades. The formulation says, with the precision Claudel was capable of and chose to use sparingly: an instant.

What complicates the case, and what the chapter has to render carefully, is that the instant of December 25, 1886 was followed by four years during which Claudel did not make his first communion as an adult, did not formally re-enter the Catholic Church, did not declare himself a Catholic in any public way. The instantaneous certainty of God, by Claudel's own account, did not produce instantaneous practice. Practice took until Christmas Day of 1890 — the fourth anniversary of the moment — for the Catholic life to formally begin. The instant was the seed. The growth was four years.

He opens the manuscript. He writes the date: *25 December 1886.*

{

• • •

}

He was eighteen. He had been in Paris for seven years, since his family had moved from Villeneuve-sur-Fère in the Aisne to the rue Madame in the sixth arrondissement. He had been at the Lycée Louis-le-Grand for the last three. He was preparing the *baccalauréat* in philosophy, with the intention of entering the École libre des sciences politiques to study for the diplomatic service. His older sister Camille was at the École des Beaux-Arts and had begun to make sculptures that the family did not quite know what to do with. His father was in the customs service. His mother was austere.

What was happening inside him, in the autumn and early winter of 1886, was a despair with the materials his education had given him. The Third Republic of his adolescence was the Republic of Renan and the post-1870 anti-clerical settlement, in which the death of God was the assumption of the educated and the official intellectual culture had organized itself around scientific positivism. Claudel had read Renan's *Vie de Jésus* with the diligence the curriculum required and had found the book hollow. He had read Hugo, the *Légende des siècles,* with admiration that did not reach the place he needed reaching. He had read the Naturalists. He had begun, in the previous summer, to read Rimbaud — the *Illuminations* and *Une Saison en enfer,* which had appeared in 1886 in the small editions Verlaine and Vanier were producing at the *Mercure de France.* Rimbaud had moved him in a way nothing else had. The Rimbaud who had written *Une Saison en enfer* was the figure of a young man for whom the available materials of the late nineteenth century were not enough, who had gone to the very edge of what the language could do and had then walked away from poetry entirely. Claudel had been reading Rimbaud for several months and had not known what to do with the reading.

What Rimbaud represented for the young Claudel was, in part, the figure of a poet who had pursued a spiritual quest outside conventional religion. At sixteen, in the famous *Lettre du Voyant* of 1871, Rimbaud had outlined his method of becoming a visionary by what he called *un long, immense et raisonné dérèglement de tous les sens* — a long, immense, and reasoned disordering of all the senses. The early poetry was virulently anti-clerical and mocking; in *Les Premières Communions* and the parish poems of 1871 he had derided small-town piety as cruelly as anyone in nineteenth-century French verse, the village churches places where ugly children fouled the pillars and the bourgeois faith of the provinces was a thin and stupid thing. And yet — this was what Claudel could see, and what he had not yet known what to do with — the same Rimbaud had remained preoccupied with God and the question of God even as he blasphemed against the available answers. The mockery and the preoccupation were two faces of the same intelligence. Rimbaud had been hunting the divine in places no respectable churchman would have looked, and had hunted with the seriousness of a man whose whole life depended on the hunt. He had stopped writing at twenty-one and gone to Africa. The figure was, for Claudel in the autumn of 1886, the figure of a quest he could not yet name and could not yet enter.

He had not, until the last weeks of 1886, been thinking about religion. He had been raised a Catholic in the formal sense — baptized, communion at twelve, confirmed — but the family practice had been minimal and had stopped, for him, in adolescence. He had not been to Mass in two or three years except on rare obligation. He was, by the conventional measure of late-nineteenth-century Parisian secular education, exactly what the Republic intended him to be: a serious young man without religious conviction, on his way into the diplomatic service.

{

• • •

}

He had attended the morning Mass at Notre-Dame on Christmas Day, with his younger sister Louise. He had not gone for any spiritual reason; he had gone, he later said, *for aesthetic reasons*, because Christmas Mass at Notre-Dame was the kind of cultural occasion an educated young Parisian was expected to attend at least once. The morning Mass had not moved him. He had described it afterward as having given him *un médiocre plaisir* — a mediocre pleasure. He had walked back home along the Quai des Grands Augustins. He had eaten the family Christmas lunch.

In the afternoon, with nothing particular to do, he had wandered back across the river to the Île de la Cité, with the vague thought that he might attend the second Vespers — the afternoon office, traditionally the great office of the day in the medieval Catholic calendar.

He arrived at Notre-Dame around four o'clock. The cathedral was full. The afternoon was already turning toward evening; the light through the rose windows was the cold blue-grey light of a Paris winter dusk. He had not been able to find a seat. He had stood at the back of the nave during the early part of the office. As the office moved into the choir's great section — the singing of the psalms, the chapter, the hymn — he had moved forward, in the way a young man without a specific seat moves through a crowd, until he had found a place to stand near the choir entrance, against the second pillar of the chancel on the north side. He could see the choir from this position. He could see the candles. He could see the cantor and the canons in their stalls.

The Magnificat began.

{

• • •

}

The Magnificat — the canticle of the Virgin Mary, *Magnificat anima mea Dominum, et exsultavit spiritus meus in Deo salutari meo* — is the great evening canticle of the Catholic liturgy. It is sung at every Vespers, every day of the year. The text is from the first chapter of the Gospel of Luke. The Virgin, having heard from the angel that she is to bear the Christ, visits her cousin Elizabeth, who is pregnant with John the Baptist; Mary's response is the song of magnification, the proclamation that the Lord has done great things in her, that the proud have been scattered and the humble exalted, that the rich have been sent empty away. The song has been set by every great composer of European sacred music. The setting at Notre-Dame on the afternoon of December 25, 1886 was the standard liturgical one — Gregorian chant, sung by the choir of canons and the cathedral choir.

What happened, when the Magnificat began, was not a sound. Or rather it was a sound — the choir was singing — but the sound was not what registered. What registered was something Claudel did not have a word for at eighteen and would not have a word for at forty-five. The closest available word, when he came to write *Ma conversion* in 1913, was *certainty.* The certainty arrived in him with the opening phrase of the Magnificat — *Magnificat anima mea Dominum* — and arrived so completely that he had no warning of it and no choice about it. He was, an instant before, an eighteen-year-old standing against a pillar in a Christmas crowd, with the despair of the Republic's positivism in him and Rimbaud unread on his table. He was, an instant after, a believer.

He did not, later, claim that he had seen anything. He did not claim that he had heard a voice. He did not claim any of the categories of supernatural experience that the older Christian tradition had given names to — vision, locution, ecstasy. What he claimed was that, in the moment between two notes of the Magnificat antiphon, the existence of God had become for him as immediate and as certain as the existence of the pillar he was standing against. The pillar was stone. God was. That was the structure of the certainty. There was no argument involved. There was nothing argued against.

He did not move from the pillar. He stayed there for the rest of Vespers — the *Magnificat* in its full setting; the Lord's Prayer; the collect; the closing. He did not weep. He did not, on examination, have any of the specific emotions that the Catholic tradition had names for. He was, simply, a different person from the person who had walked into Notre-Dame an hour before. The difference was complete, and would, by his own subsequent account, never reverse.

When Vespers ended he walked out of the cathedral into the cold grey afternoon. The lamps were beginning to be lit on the Quai aux Fleurs. He walked slowly across the Pont Notre-Dame and along the Quai de la Mégisserie and across the Pont des Arts and home. He did not say anything to anyone. When he arrived at the rue Madame his sister Louise asked him whether he had enjoyed the Vespers. He said yes. He went up to his room and sat at his desk for a long time.

{

• • •

}

The four years that followed were not what either he or the moment might have predicted. The moment had given him certainty. The certainty had not given him a practice. He did not begin going to Mass regularly. He did not begin taking communion. He did not present himself to a priest. He read. He read the New Testament in the small Latin Vulgate he had bought for the purpose. He read the *Imitation of Christ*. He read Pascal. He continued, with even more attention, to read Rimbaud. He continued at the Lycée. He took the *baccalauréat*. He entered the École libre des sciences politiques.

What was being worked out, in those four years, was the question of practice. The certainty was not a question. The certainty was a fact of his life as fixed as his height. The question was what, given the certainty, the rest of the life had to look like. He resisted, for those four years, the answer the Catholic Church would have given him. He resisted the formal practice. He did not believe the answer was wrong; he believed he was not yet ready for it. He needed the four years.

On Christmas Day 1890, four years to the day after the moment, he made his first adult confession, with Abbé Villaume, and received communion at the midnight Mass at Notre-Dame — returning, at his own quiet insistence, to the cathedral in which the moment had occurred. The four-year integration was complete. The remainder of his life would be lived inside the Catholic Church, with the discipline he had resisted now accepted in full.

{

• • •

}

The diplomatic career began in 1893 with a posting to the French consulate in New York and continued for the next forty-two years. He served in China — fourteen years, the longest single posting; in Prague; in Frankfurt; in Hamburg; in Rome; in Rio; in Tokyo, where he was ambassador during the great Kantō earthquake of September 1923; in Copenhagen; in Brussels. He retired from the diplomatic service in 1935, at sixty-seven. He had been writing throughout — the great plays *Partage de Midi* (1906), *L'Annonce faite à Marie* (1912), *Le Soulier de satin* (1924); the *Cinq Grandes Odes* (1910); the long essays of biblical exegesis in the years after his retirement.

He married Reine Sainte-Marie-Perrin in 1906. They had five children. The marriage was not the marriage he had originally hoped for; he had been, in 1900-1901, in a passionate liaison with a married woman he met aboard ship, Rosalie Vetch, who bore him a daughter and then returned to her husband. The affair was the material that became *Partage de Midi*. He had, after several years of suffering, married Reine and accepted the marriage as a vocation rather than as a romance.

His sister Camille, the sculptor — Rodin's lover and student through the 1880s and 1890s — was institutionalized in 1913 by their mother and Paul, after the breakdown that was probably a psychotic illness. She remained institutionalized for thirty years, until her death in 1943. Paul visited her infrequently. The relationship, which has been the subject of considerable revisionist criticism in the late twentieth century, was complicated by everything that complicated it.

Claudel collaborated with composers — Darius Milhaud (*Christophe Colomb*, 1928, and many other works), Arthur Honegger (*Jeanne d'Arc au bûcher*, 1938; *La Danse des morts*, 1938) — and produced some of the great twentieth-century French oratorio texts. He was elected to the Académie française in 1946 at seventy-eight.

He died in Paris on February 23, 1955, at eighty-six. He was given a state funeral at Notre-Dame — the same cathedral in which the moment had occurred sixty-eight years earlier — and was buried at his estate at Brangues in the Isère.

{

• • •

}

Daniel sets the manuscript aside. The Claudel chapter has been the chapter of the instant. Pascal had two hours. Claudel had a fraction of a second — the fraction between the cantor's intoning of the *Magnificat* antiphon and the choir's response. The fraction was sufficient.

What strikes Daniel about Claudel, on rereading the chapter, is the gap between the moment and the practice. The moment, by Claudel's testimony, was instantaneous. The practice took four years. The conversion that Claudel claimed in *Ma conversion* of 1913 had been a single moment was, on closer examination, a single moment plus four years of integration. The four years are the part of the conversion that the famous formula does not contain. The instant gave the certainty. The four years gave the life. Both were necessary.

For Daniel, who is not in the business of providing certainty in his own case, the chapter is a study of a phenomenon that does not, in the lawyerly sense, admit of cross-examination. The moment in Notre-Dame is what Claudel reported. The reporting is consistent across decades. The life that followed is consistent with the reporting. Daniel does not, as he did not with Pascal, credit the metaphysical claim. He does, as with Pascal, recognize that something happened in that man at that pillar at that moment, and that the something organized the rest of the life. The structure of the testimony is solid. The interpretation of what was being testified to is the part Daniel cannot enter.

What Daniel notes, with the small fairness he tries to maintain through these chapters, is that Claudel's certainty held. It did not, across sixty-eight years and a long diplomatic career and a complicated personal life, weaken. *Aucun livre, aucun raisonnement, aucun hasard d'une vie agitée n'ont pu ébranler ma foi, ni à vrai dire la toucher.* No book, no reasoning, no chance of an agitated life has been able to shake my faith or, truly, to touch it. The line is from *Ma conversion*. It is not the kind of line one writes lightly. It is also not the kind of line that the late twentieth and twenty-first centuries have been entirely comfortable with — the secular educated reader hears in it a kind of intransigence that the modern liberal-Catholic settlement has tried to soften. Claudel did not soften. The certainty had been given to him whole. He gave it back in the same form for the rest of his life.

He closes the notebook. He goes to the listening chair. He chooses, this evening, Bach's *Magnificat in D*, BWV 243, in the John Eliot Gardiner recording with the English Baroque Soloists. The opening burst — *Magnificat anima mea Dominum* — comes up out of the orchestra in the way Bach wrote it, with the brilliance of the trumpets and the joy of the chorus. It is not the Magnificat that was sung at Notre-Dame on December 25, 1886; that was the chant. It is, however, the Magnificat as the European tradition has continued to sing it, with the same words and the same theological claim, in every generation since.

Figures at the Threshold

Rosenzweig

Daniel sits at the desk. The Rosenzweig materials are out: *Der Stern der Erlösung* (The Star of Redemption) in the German edition and the William Hallo translation; the *Briefe und Tagebücher* in two volumes; the small *Understanding the Sick and the Healthy*; the Glatzer biography; the Galli edition of the conversion correspondence; the small Schocken volume of selected essays. He has been working on Rosenzweig for two weeks.

Rosenzweig is the great un-conversion. He represents — alone among the figures in the book so far — the type in which the threshold is approached, the foot is on the step, and the figure turns around. He is the formal counterpoint to every Christian convert in the collection, and the formal answer to Spinoza across two hundred and fifty-seven years. Spinoza had been thrown out of his Sephardic community in Amsterdam in 1656; Rosenzweig in Berlin in 1913 was about to leave the Ashkenazi community of his German-Jewish bourgeois family voluntarily, by his own choice, on what he believed at the time to be sufficient intellectual grounds. He was, on the morning of October 11, 1913, two weeks away from being baptized as a Lutheran. He did not become a Lutheran. He became, in the day that followed, the figure he had been on his way to ceasing to be — a Jew, observant, philosophically committed, and the author over the next sixteen years of one of the most important works of twentieth-century Jewish thought.

The day was Yom Kippur — the Day of Atonement, the holiest day of the Jewish calendar, the fast-day that closes the High Holy Days. He spent it in a small Orthodox synagogue in Berlin. He had gone in as a man preparing to leave. He came out as a man who could not leave. The letter to his cousin Rudolf Ehrenberg three weeks later contained the formula that would, eventually, become famous: *It seems no longer necessary; and indeed, in my case, no longer possible.*

What the chapter has to render is the day itself. The intellectual reasoning that brought him to the eve of conversion is well documented. The day in the synagogue is less so; Rosenzweig, with the discretion of a man for whom religious experience was real, did not publish a *Ma conversion* in the manner of Claudel. What we have is the letter, *The Star of Redemption* in which the day is everywhere implicit and nowhere explicit, and the small body of testimony from those who knew him before and after October 1913.

He writes the date at the top of the page: *11 October 1913.*

{

• • •

}

He was twenty-six. He had been born on Christmas Day 1886 in Kassel, into a wealthy and assimilated German-Jewish family.

The household was observant in the Reform sense — which in cultivated German-Jewish bourgeois houses by the 1890s meant attending the High Holy Days services and very little else. The family kept a kosher kitchen but a non-kosher table in the dining room. They did not study Hebrew. They thought of themselves as German citizens of the Mosaic confession, in the formula of the period.

He had studied medicine briefly, then turned to history and philosophy. He had completed his doctorate, on *Hegel and the State*, under Friedrich Meinecke at Berlin in 1912. The dissertation was a major work; published in 1920 as *Hegel und der Staat* it would establish him as a serious figure in German philosophical scholarship before he was thirty.

His cousins on the Ehrenberg side were the formative figures of his intellectual life. Hans Ehrenberg, his older cousin, had converted to Lutheran Christianity in 1909 and become a Protestant theologian. Eugen Rosenstock-Huessy, also a cousin, was a younger man of brilliance, a Christian, who would go on to a major American career after fleeing Nazi Germany. The two of them, with another cousin Rudolf Ehrenberg, had formed the *Patmos Circle* — a small group of German Christians and German Jews who had been writing to each other about religious and philosophical questions since their student days.

In July 1913 Rosenzweig had spent a night arguing with Rosenstock-Huessy in Leipzig. The argument had run from after dinner to dawn. It had ended with Rosenzweig conceding what he had been resisting for years — that the modern educated mind could not, in any serious sense, remain a *pagan*; that the religious question was, for the modern intellect, the Christian question; and that he, Franz Rosenzweig, would have to convert.

He had communicated the decision to his mother and to Rudolf Ehrenberg. He had begun the formal preparation.

What the cousins had insisted on, and what Rosenzweig had accepted, was that he must convert *as a Jew, not as a pagan.* He must know what he was leaving before he could leave it. He must, in the months before the baptism, attend the High Holy Days services in the Jewish manner. He must read what he had not read of the Jewish tradition. He was twenty-six; he had not had a Jewish education; he was about to leave Judaism for Christianity, and the conditions of leaving — imposed on him by his Christian cousins, who had thought about this longer than he had — required him first to understand the country he was leaving.

{

• • •

}

He had attended Rosh Hashanah at his family's Reform synagogue in Kassel — polished, partly in German, with a choir and an organ. For Yom Kippur he chose a small Orthodox synagogue in Berlin instead — a *shtibel* in an older Jewish neighborhood, holding perhaps eighty men.

The Kol Nidre service on the evening of October 10 was his first sustained encounter with Orthodox liturgy. The Aramaic was unfamiliar. The cantor was an old man in a white *kittel*, the burial-shroud robe of the High Holy Days. He went home and did not sleep well.

The day began at sunrise. He took the seat the *gabbai* had reserved for him and put on the tallit one of his cousins had given him in preparation. The morning service was long. The Hebrew was not a language he knew; he followed in a German *machzor*. As the morning went on, the translation was not adequate to what was happening in the Hebrew. The Hebrew was older. The Hebrew had a weight the German did not.

The Avodah came at the climax of the morning — the long retelling of the High Priest's service in the Second Temple on Yom Kippur. At three points in the recitation, the congregation fell prostrate on the floor — the only prostration in the entire Jewish liturgical year. Rosenzweig had not been told this would happen. He went to the floor with the men around him.

When he stood up he was not the man who had gone down.

{

• • •

}

The afternoon passed in the slow descent of the day's energy. The fast was in his body.

Ne'ilah began at sunset — the closing of the gates, the final service, the moment when the gates of judgment close. The cantor's voice had been worn thin by the day. The final prayer was the *Shema Yisrael*, recited with an intensity Rosenzweig had not known the prayer was capable of. *Hear, O Israel, the Lord our God, the Lord is One.* The line was repeated three times. Then *Adonai hu ha-Elohim* — the Lord, He is God — repeated seven times, the cantor's broken voice leading.

Then the shofar. The *tekiah gedolah*, the single long blast, closed the day.

The men began to greet each other. *Gut yontiff.* The lights were being turned up.

Rosenzweig stood without moving. He was no longer the man who had walked into the synagogue the previous evening. He had attempted to know Judaism in order to leave it. The knowing had taken him, against his expectation, into the country.

He walked back to his lodgings through the cooling Berlin night. He broke his fast alone. He did not write to anyone for three weeks.

{

• • •

}

On October 31, 1913, he wrote to Rudolf Ehrenberg. The letter has survived. It is one of the founding documents of twentieth-century Jewish self-understanding. Rosenzweig explained, with the care of a young philosopher who knew his cousin would need to be persuaded by reasoning rather than testimony, what had happened to him at Yom Kippur and what it meant for the planned conversion.

He could no longer convert. His earlier reasoning had been correct in everything it had said about the impossibility of paganism, and incorrect only in the conclusion it had drawn. The conclusion had been that Christianity was the only available answer for the modern intellect. The day in the small Orthodox synagogue had shown him that Judaism was also an available answer — not as the survival of a culture, which his Reform upbringing had given him, but as the living religious form he had been preparing to leave.

The famous formulation came in the letter: *It seems no longer necessary; and indeed, in my case, no longer possible.*

He continued to correspond with Rosenstock-Huessy and the Ehrenbergs for the rest of his life. The Christians did not abandon him; he did not abandon them. His later work — *The Star of Redemption* most centrally — was the philosophical articulation of a position in which Judaism and Christianity were two equally valid covenants, addressed to different peoples, both true, both necessary, neither reducible to the other.

{

• • •

}

The First World War took him into the Austro-Hungarian army on the Balkan front. He served in an anti-aircraft unit. He wrote *Der Stern der Erlösung* — *The Star of Redemption* — on field postcards in 1918, sending them home to his mother for safekeeping. The work was assembled into a book and published in 1921. It is one of the most demanding philosophical works of the twentieth century, and one of the most influential works of twentieth-century Jewish thought; Levinas would later say he had read it on every Sabbath of his adult life.

He returned to Frankfurt after the war. He founded the *Freies Jüdisches Lehrhaus* — the Free Jewish House of Learning — in 1920, an institution for the adult Jewish education of assimilated German Jews who had lost the Jewish learning of their ancestors and wanted, in their own version of the path Rosenzweig had walked, to recover it. The Lehrhaus became a major institution of Weimar Jewish life. Buber, Erich Fromm, Leo Strauss, Gershom Scholem, and many others taught there.

He married Edith Hahn in 1920. They had a son, Rafael, born 1922.

In late 1921 he began to lose function in his hands. By early 1922 the diagnosis was amyotrophic lateral sclerosis — Lou Gehrig's disease — a progressive paralysis that would be fatal within a few years. He was thirty-five.

The seven years that followed are among the most extraordinary in modern intellectual history. Rosenzweig progressively lost the use of his arms, his legs, his voice, and finally his ability to write. His wife Edith devised a system: she would say the letters of the alphabet, he would blink at the correct letter, and the words and sentences and pages would assemble themselves slowly. Through this system — and through the love of the woman who operated it — he continued to compose. He worked, with Martin Buber, on the German translation of the Hebrew Bible — the Buber-Rosenzweig Bible — which is one of the great translations in any modern European language. He wrote essays on translation, on Yehuda Halevi, on Jewish education, on the structure of Jewish prayer.

He died in Frankfurt on December 10, 1929, at forty-two. The day he died he had been working, with Edith, on a translation. The work was within sight of completion when he stopped.

{

• • •

}

Daniel sets the manuscript aside. The Rosenzweig chapter has been the chapter of the un-conversion — the figure who answered the great Christian conversion of the modern period not by conversion in the other direction but by the discovery that he had been about to leave a country he did not yet know.

What strikes Daniel about Rosenzweig is the precision. The threshold was real; the foot had been on the step; the baptism had been scheduled. The day in the small Orthodox synagogue had not been planned as a turning point; it had been planned as the preparation for departure. The turning was something the day produced; Rosenzweig had not produced it. *It seems no longer necessary; and indeed, in my case, no longer possible.* The line is precise. He did not say that Christianity was wrong, or that his cousins had been wrong, or that the reasoning of July 1913 had been mistaken. He said that the conversion had become, in his particular case, no longer possible. The possibility had been removed by the day.

What Daniel notes, with the small comparative attention he has been bringing to the religious geography of the book, is that the Jewish-to-Christian boundary has different textures depending on which Judaism and which Christianity. Spinoza's community in 1656 had been Sephardic — Portuguese exiles in Amsterdam, with the Inquisition still in family memory, and the boundary across which a Sephardic Jew might be expelled or might convert had run for centuries through Catholicism, through the Iberian and Mediterranean Catholic world. Rosenzweig's community in 1913 was Ashkenazi — Central European bourgeois Reform Judaism of the post-Napoleonic emancipation — and the boundary across which he was about to step ran through Lutheranism, through the German Protestant confession and the philosophical inheritance of Luther and Hegel and the German universities. The Sephardic and Ashkenazi paths had not been the same path; the Catholic and Lutheran destinations had not been the same destination. Rosenzweig was answering Spinoza, but the answer was not in the same language Spinoza had refused to speak.

This is the most philosophically interesting form of the Jewish-Christian boundary the book contains. Rosenzweig did not argue that one tradition was true and the other false. He argued that both were true; that they spoke to different peoples; that the covenant given to Israel at Sinai was as real as the covenant given to the church at Pentecost; that the modern Jew who had been about to leave Judaism for Christianity was therefore not crossing from falsity to truth but moving from one truth to another, and that the moving was not, after Yom Kippur 1913, possible for him. He had been given a country. He could not leave it.

There is a complication, Daniel notes, in Rosenzweig's claim that the modern educated mind cannot remain pagan. The claim was true, perhaps, for the German intellectual world of 1913 — formed by the long inheritance of Kant and Hegel and Schelling, in which the religious question was the question every serious mind had to confront. It has become less true in the century since. The educated mind of the early twenty-first century — Daniel's mind, and the mind of the secular intellectual culture in which he has lived for sixty years — has organized itself around methodological agnosticism, scientific naturalism, and a pluralism that does not require any choice between traditions. The religious question, for this mind, is a question about other people's beliefs, not a live question the educated must answer. Paganism, in the looser sense in which Rosenzweig's cousins used the word, has turned out to be possible after all — as a stable position, at any rate, for the duration of one well-examined life. Whether it is possible across the longer course of a civilization is a different question, and one Daniel does not pretend to be able to answer. For himself, in his own time, in his own apartment, the position has held.

For Daniel — the reader who has been holding the position of the educated secular agnostic through nine chapters — the Rosenzweig case is the one that, paradoxically, most respects his own settlement. Rosenzweig did not require that Daniel choose between traditions. Rosenzweig allowed for the structure in which different peoples were addressed by different religious forms, and in which the universal rational settlement Daniel inhabited could be one further form, addressed to its own population, neither superior nor inferior to the others. The Rosenzweigian frame is, in Daniel's reading, the most generous philosophical frame the book has yet encountered. He should add, in fairness, that he is not a reader of the Hebrew Bible or of the theological literature; the categories of covenant and people that Rosenzweig was thinking in are not categories Daniel has himself been thinking in. He has been thinking in his own secular Spinozist register. What Rosenzweig's frame does, in Daniel's case, is to grant that register a place at the table without requiring Daniel to be the kind of reader he has not been.

What Daniel finds himself thinking about most, however, when he closes the chapter, is the part of Rosenzweig's life he had not, on first reading, expected to find moving. The seven years of progressive paralysis from 1922 to 1929 are the most extraordinary part of the biography. A man of thirty-five, with a major work just published, with the founding of the Lehrhaus a year behind him, with a wife and a son not yet a year old, is told by his physicians that he has a progressive disease that will paralyze him completely and kill him within a few years. He responds by continuing to work — by inventing, with Edith, a system of communication that allows him to dictate by blinking at letters; by translating the Hebrew Bible with Buber over those years; by composing essays that some readers consider his finest writing.

He turns the dying into a continuous composition.

Daniel is seventy-eight. He does not have ALS. He has, in the actuarial sense, perhaps three to ten more good working years, depending on luck and the cardiologist. He is not, in the way Rosenzweig was at thirty-five, suddenly confronting the question of how to work in a body that is failing. He is confronting the slower question, which is how to work in a body that is, by its own steady calendar, drawing closer to the moment when work will no longer be possible. Rosenzweig had the harder version. Daniel has the softer one. The lesson Daniel takes from the harder version is the lesson it ought to be possible to take: that the work continues for as long as the means of working can be improvised, and that the means can be improvised further than one would have predicted before the test arrives. Edith Rosenzweig's alphabet, blink by blink, is the exemplary case of the means improvised further than expected. Daniel notes it. He notes also that Edith was the irreducible condition of the system, and that he himself, having lost Marie-Claire three years ago, would not have access to the Edith-version of the means, and that his version of Rosenzweig's last seven years would, if it ever came, be performed alone.

He closes the notebook. He goes to the listening chair. He chooses, this evening, Max Bruch's *Kol Nidrei*, op. 47, in the recording by Jacqueline du Pré with the Israel Philharmonic under Daniel Barenboim. Bruch was not Jewish; the *Kol Nidrei* was written in 1880 in Liverpool, on themes Bruch had received from a Berlin cantor. It is the German-Jewish cultural artifact that captures, in the cello's voice, the prayer that opens Yom Kippur and that Rosenzweig had heard for the first time in the small Berlin synagogue on the evening of October 10, 1913. The cello begins. The orchestra answers. The melody rises.

Figures at the Threshold

Conze

Daniel sits at the desk. The Conze materials are out: *Buddhism: Its Essence and Development* (Cassirer, 1951); *Buddhist Thought in India* (1962); the *Aṣṭasāhasrikā Prajñāpāramitā* in the Conze translation; *Buddhist Wisdom Books* — Conze's combined translation of the *Diamond Sutra* and *Heart Sutra*; the posthumous *Memoirs of a Modern Gnostic* in two volumes. He has been working on Conze for two weeks.

Conze is the conversion-by-reading. He represents — alone among the figures in the book — the type in which the entire turning happens in the silence of a room with books open on a desk, without ceremony, without community, without a single dateable moment of crossing. There was no Pansil at Galle. There was no kneeling by a fire. There was no Magnificat in a cathedral. Conze had arrived at his Buddhism by reading, by translating, by sitting alone in libraries with the Sanskrit and the Pali and the Chinese open in front of him, and the question of when exactly he had become a Buddhist was a question he himself, in his autobiographical writings, treated as having no precise answer.

The chapter is therefore formally different from the others. It cannot compress around a single hour or a single day. It compresses, instead, around an interval — roughly the years from 1937 to 1942, when Conze in London moved out of his Marxist phase, through a brief astrology-and-occult period, into the serious Buddhist study that would occupy the rest of his life. The chapter privileges a specific moment within that interval — his sustained encounter with the *Heart Sutra* during the war years — but the moment is anchored within a slower process rather than in itself.

Daniel notes that this is, of all the cases in the book, the case closest to his own intellectual life. Daniel has been a reader for sixty years. His own intellectual development has happened in the silence of rooms with books open on desks. The Conze chapter, in this sense, is the chapter that most illuminates Daniel's own way of working. And yet Conze, unlike Daniel, did arrive somewhere. The reading took Conze to Buddhism. It did not take Daniel anywhere. The reason for the difference is the chapter's quiet question.

He writes the date at the top of the page: *London, 1939–1942.*

{

• • •

}

Edward Conze had been born in London on March 18, 1904, into a complicated Anglo-German-Indian family. His father Ernst was a German vice-consul in London. His mother Adele was English with German connections of her own. His paternal grandfather had been a German diplomat married to a Bengali woman; the Indian thread, which Conze cultivated in later life as part of his self-presentation, ran through that grandmother. The family moved back to Germany when Edward was a child; he grew up speaking German, was educated in German universities, and considered himself German until he was thirty.

He had studied at Tübingen, Heidelberg, Kiel, and Cologne. At Cologne in 1928 he completed a doctorate on the principle of contradiction — a phenomenological treatment of the question that would become, in revised form, his first book. He had heard Husserl lecture at Freiburg; he had been formed by the Husserlian project of returning philosophy to the rigorous description of consciousness. He had also been formed, like every serious German student of his generation, by Hegel and Kant and the long Idealist inheritance, and by the philosophical seriousness that the German universities of the Weimar period produced.

By the late 1920s he had become a committed Marxist. He wrote for socialist publications. He took to the streets. He believed, with the confidence of a young man who has the philosophical training of his time, that the Marxist analysis was the correct analysis of the human situation and that the historical task of his generation was to bring it to political fulfillment.

The rise of Nazism interrupted all of this. Conze, with his partial Jewish ancestry, his Marxist activity, and his English birth, was an obvious target. He fled Germany in 1933 and returned to England, where he had not lived since infancy. He took British citizenship. He worked as a tutor, as a journalist, as a part-time lecturer at the University of London Extension. He lived in furnished rooms. He was not poor in any absolute sense, but he was never again what the German bourgeoisie of his birth had been.

What happened to him in the second half of the 1930s — between roughly 1936 and 1939 — was a slow disintegration of the Marxist confidence. The historical events that disintegrated it are the historical events that disintegrated most serious Marxist confidence in that period: the Stalinist purges, the show trials, the Spanish Civil War's Republican defeat, the Hitler-Stalin pact of August 1939. Conze, like Koestler and Silone and Orwell, found that the framework he had inhabited could not survive the world the framework had failed to predict.

He cast about. In one of the small autobiographical confessions of his later writings, he admitted that for a brief period in 1937 and 1938 he had taken up astrology — not as a public position but as a private practice, looking for an organizing system to replace the Marxism that had failed him. He cast horoscopes. He read the occult literature that was more readily available in interwar London than it had been at Heidelberg. The astrology was not, he later said, satisfactory; but it had been the gateway through which he came to the Eastern texts — for the late-Victorian and Edwardian English occult literature, which he had been reading in his crisis period, was thoroughly impregnated with garbled Indian and Buddhist material, and the garbled material had pointed him toward the originals.

{

• • •

}

He began reading Buddhist texts in earnest in 1939. The texts available in English translation were a mixed body: the Pali Canon translations of T. W. Rhys Davids and the Pali Text Society — uneven, often Victorian in their religiosity, but the only access to the early texts; D. T. Suzuki's *Essays in Zen Buddhism* in three volumes, which had introduced Zen to Western readers; the Stcherbatsky translations from the Buddhist logical school, which were rigorously philosophical and which interested Conze especially. He read all of this. He began, in 1940, to study Sanskrit seriously — taking lessons from a private tutor in London, working through the grammars, approaching the texts in their original language.

What he found in the Buddhist texts was the philosophy he had been looking for. The Husserlian rigor was there, in the early Abhidharma analyses of consciousness. The dialectical structure was there, in the Mahayana negation of self-existent entities. The phenomenological description of mental events was, in the Theravada *Visuddhimagga,* more careful than anything in the Western tradition. The metaphysical critique of substance was, in the Madhyamaka of Nagarjuna, more thorough than anything Husserl had attempted. Buddhism, as Conze read it in those London rooms in 1940 and 1941, was a complete philosophical system that addressed the questions his German training had taught him to ask, with a rigor his German training had not led him to expect from Asian sources.

He met other Buddhists. Christmas Humphreys, the founder of the Buddhist Society, had an office in central London; Conze visited him several times, found him intellectually slight, and kept his distance. He attended some of the evenings at the Society. He did not take to the social side of British Buddhism. His Buddhism was, from the beginning, primarily a textual project — not a spiritual community.

The war was overhead. London was being bombed in 1940 and 1941; Conze worked through the Blitz in his rented rooms, sometimes in basements, with the Sanskrit texts and the dictionaries on the small writing-table in front of him. He had, by 1942, decided that he would devote his scholarly life to the *Prajñāpāramitā* — the *Perfection of Wisdom* literature of the Mahayana, the philosophical core of the Mahayana tradition, which had been almost untranslated into English. The decision was not made in a moment. The decision crystallized across some weeks of reading and rereading and finding that this was the body of texts that addressed him with the most immediacy.

{

• • •

}

Within the Prajñāpāramitā literature, the *Heart Sutra* is the shortest text. It is also the most concentrated. The full text in Sanskrit runs to less than three hundred syllables; in English translation it occupies less than a printed page. It is recited daily in Mahayana monasteries from Tibet to Japan. It is the text through which most Western students of the Mahayana first encounter the doctrine of *śūnyatā* — emptiness — which is the central philosophical claim of the tradition.

Conze worked on the *Heart Sutra* extensively from the early 1940s onward. The translation he eventually published in *Buddhist Wisdom Books* in 1958, alongside his translation of the *Diamond Sutra*, was the result of nearly two decades of textual work. But the first sustained encounter with the text had taken place in those London years. He had a Sanskrit edition. He had the Chinese versions of Kumārajīva and Xuanzang for comparison. He had the Tibetan translation. He had the small Pali Canon precedents for some of the formulas.

The text turns on the formula in its heart: *rūpaṁ śūnyatā śūny-*

ataiva rūpam — form is emptiness, emptiness is form. The formula extends through the five skandhas — feeling, perception, mental formations, consciousness — each in turn declared to be emptiness, and emptiness declared to be each of them. The formula refuses, with the systematic insistence of a philosophical text, the attempt to locate any of the five aggregates of experience as a self-existent thing. There is no self. There is no thing that is not also an absence. There is no absence that is not also a thing.

What Conze understood, in working through the formula in those London years, was that *śūnyatā* was not mysticism. It was a philosophical position. It was, specifically, a position about the relational nature of all experience — that nothing in experience can be picked out as having self-existence; that what we call *form* is only intelligible because of what we call *emptiness*, and vice versa; that the categorial structure of consciousness is, in the deepest analysis, a structure of mutual constitution rather than substance. The Husserlian in Conze recognized the structure. The Madhyamaka critique of substance was, he came to think, what Husserlian phenomenology had been groping toward without quite reaching.

The recognition was the moment, if there was a moment. It was not dramatic. He was sitting at a desk in a rented room in London, in the early 1940s, with the Sanskrit text in front of him and the Chinese versions to one side and his own draft translation in pencil on a sheet of foolscap. He read the formula. He understood it. He did not stand up. He did not weep. He did not make any of the gestures that the converts of the other chapters had made. He continued working. The work continued for the next thirty years.

{

• • •

}

The decade of the 1940s was the decade in which Conze became Conze. He completed *Buddhism: Its Essence and Development,* which Cassirer published in 1951 — the small book that introduced Buddhism to a generation of educated English readers, which is still in print, and which is considered by serious scholars one of the most reliable popular introductions to the tradition ever written. He continued the *Prajñāpāramitā* work. He produced, in the next thirty years, what is by general agreement the major body of Western translations from the Mahayana — the *Aṣṭasāhasrikā Prajñāpāramitā* in 1958 and the longer versions in subsequent decades, the *Diamond Sutra* and *Heart Sutra* in 1958, *Selected Sayings from the Perfection of Wisdom,* the *Buddhist Texts Through the Ages* anthology with co-editors. He wrote *Buddhist Thought in India* in 1962, a more rigorous academic treatment of Mahayana philosophy, which is the single book on which his scholarly reputation rests.

He married twice; the first marriage failed; the second held until his death. He held visiting positions at Lancaster, Bonn, the University of Washington, and elsewhere. He never had a permanent academic chair. He lived in modest circumstances all his life.

He became, in his late years, an eccentric and increasingly difficult figure. He developed reactionary political views — racially conservative, occasionally antisemitic in his comments, despite his own partial Jewish ancestry, hostile to the post-1968 academic left. The autobiographical *Memoirs of a Modern Gnostic,* published posthumously in 1979, contains some statements that have made his later admirers uncomfortable. His Buddhism remained serious throughout; the political views did not impair the scholarship; but the figure of the late Conze is not, on the personal level, an attractive one.

He died on September 24, 1979, at seventy-five, in the south of England. The translations continue to be reprinted. They are read.

{

• • •

}

Daniel sets the manuscript aside. The Conze chapter has been the chapter of the conversion-by-reading. There was no Pansil. There was no kneeling. There was no Magnificat. The conversion happened in rooms with books open on desks, alone, across years, by the slow accumulation of philosophical understanding, in a man whose entire prior philosophical training — Husserl, Hegel, the German universities — turned out to have prepared him for the encounter without his knowing.

What Daniel notes, when he sets the chapter in its larger context, is that Conze was not the first serious German engagement with Buddhism. Schopenhauer had been there a century earlier — reading the Latin *Oupnek'hat* translation of the Upanishads every night before bed for the last thirty years of his life, calling the book the consolation of his life and the consolation of his death, keeping a small statue of the Buddha in his study at Frankfurt. He was not a convert; he was a philosopher who had recognized convergence. He had, however, prepared the German philosophical ear for what Conze would later make audible in translation. Between Schopenhauer and Conze stood Hermann Hesse — the Swabian-Swiss novelist, son of a

Pietist missionary who had served in India, whose *Siddhartha* of 1922 introduced more Western readers to Buddhist and Hindu sensibility than any other twentieth-century book. Hesse had not converted either. His Buddhism was literary; he died in 1962 a Swiss novelist with a Nobel Prize, not a Buddhist. But he had been, like Schopenhauer, a fellow-traveler. The German engagement with Buddhism, from Schopenhauer through Hesse to Conze, had moved from philosophical recognition through literary popularization to scholarly translation. Conze had been the third generation.

What also draws Daniel to the Conze case, on reflection, is that the philosophical Buddhism Conze translated has surprising affinities with several principles Daniel has held throughout his life. The Buddhist tradition makes the person responsible for their own liberation: there is no external savior, no proxy that can do the work, no community that can substitute for the work. The famous late instruction attributed to the Buddha — *be islands unto yourselves, refuges unto yourselves, with no external refuge* — could almost have been a sentence of nineteenth-century liberal individualism. Personal responsibility compatible with inner freedom. Self-reliance — individualism, in the constitutional sense Daniel has lived with for fifty years. Respect for the person and for pluralism, with one exception: for extremism, for the position that demands the displacement of all other positions, for the tolerance that is asked to extend to the intolerant. Liberal individualism draws its line there; the Buddhist tradition, with its emphasis on the middle way and its long history of doctrinal pluralism alongside its refusal to absolutize, draws its line in roughly the same place. Daniel finds the convergence reassuring. He does not find it converting.

What strikes Daniel about the Conze case is its specific resemblance to his own life. Daniel has been a reader for sixty years. The Constant volumes on the third shelf, the Spinoza on the second, the Bergson, the Tocqueville, the long shelves of nineteenth- and twentieth-century philosophy and history that line the apartment, are the residue of those sixty years of reading. The reading has produced in Daniel a particular kind of mind — careful, comparative, slow — and the mind has not, however, taken him to a Buddhism, or to any other religious tradition, in the way the same kind of reading took Conze.

Why not? Daniel has been turning the question over. He has not read what Conze read. He has not, at any point in his life, sat with the *Heart Sutra* in front of him and worked through the *śūnyatā* formula in Sanskrit. He does not know Sanskrit. He does not know Pali. The whole apparatus of textual access that Conze built for himself over thirty years is an apparatus Daniel has not built. This is one reason. It is not the whole reason.

The other reason, when Daniel examines it honestly, is that he has not been looking for a system to which his reading might lead. Conze had been looking. After the failure of Marxism, after the brief astrological detour, after the disintegration of the political certainties of his Weimar years, Conze had been a man looking for an organizing structure to replace the structures that had failed him. He found one. Daniel has not been looking for one. Daniel had Marie-Claire and the constitutional law and the Beacon Court apartment and the long evenings of music; the structures that organized his life were not the kind that could fail in the way Conze's had failed. He had not, in other words, had the crisis that the conversion would have answered.

This is, Daniel thinks, the small but real difference between

Conze the convert and Daniel the reader. The reading is the same. The crisis is not the same. The reading without the crisis produces a different kind of mind — Daniel's mind, which has read for sixty years and has not, at any point, found that the reading was leading toward something on which the rest of the life had to be reorganized.

He closes the notebook. He goes to the listening chair. He chooses, this evening, the recording of the *Heart Sutra* chanted in Sanskrit by Imee Ooi — the Malaysian Buddhist composer-performer whose recordings are among the most widely known of the Mahayana sutras in the international Buddhist community. The recording is not classical music in the sense Daniel has been listening to classical music for fifty years. It is, however, the *Heart Sutra* — the same text Conze worked on through the London years and translated in 1958 — being recited in the language Conze had taught himself in order to read it. Daniel listens. The voices begin: *Gate gate pāragate pārasaṁgate bodhi svāhā.* Gone, gone, gone beyond, gone altogether beyond, awakening, hail.

Figures at the Threshold

Schoenberg

Daniel sits at the desk. The Schoenberg materials are out: the *Style and Idea* essays in the Schirmer edition; the *Letters* in the Hahn translation in two volumes; the Stuckenschmidt biography; Allen Shawn's *Schoenberg's Journey*; the libretto of *Moses und Aron* in the Penguin edition with the score; the Stein collection of correspondence; recordings of *Kol Nidre* op. 39 and *A Survivor from Warsaw* op. 46 on the small shelf next to the listening chair. He has been working on Schoenberg for two weeks.

Schoenberg is the chapter of the return. He represents — alongside Rosenzweig in 1913 — the type in which the figure stays within or returns to Judaism rather than crossing into Christianity. But Schoenberg is, in a way Rosenzweig is not, the doubled case. Schoenberg had crossed once; he had been baptized Lutheran in Vienna in March 1898 at twenty-three, in the Heine pattern, with Zemlinsky as witness, in the assimilation conversion of the educated Viennese Jew who wanted a German cultural career and who was still living in the world the Heine letter to Moser had inhabited a century earlier. He had remained nominally Christian for thirty-five years. In 1933, when history demanded a different answer, he returned. The return was formalized in a small ceremony at the Liberal Synagogue at 24 rue Copernic in Paris on July 24, 1933, with Marc Chagall and Dmitri Marianoff as witnesses. He had been in Paris for about six weeks, having fled Berlin after his dismissal from the Prussian Academy of Arts on racial grounds in May.

The chapter is therefore a chapter of two conversions. The first — the 1898 Lutheran baptism — was the European-Jewish assimilation conversion in its standard form, performed for reasons Schoenberg himself in retrospect treated as having been less than fully serious. The second — the 1933 return — was the more serious one, in the sense that it answered to a historical pressure no one in 1898 could have predicted and aligned the formal religious identity with what Schoenberg had been thinking and writing for at least a decade. The 1923 letter to Kandinsky in which Schoenberg broke off the friendship over Kandinsky's antisemitism — *I am a Jew* — had been the interior return. The 1933 ceremony was the public seal.

He writes the date at the top of the page: *24 July 1933.*

{

• • •

}

He had been born in Vienna in 1874 into an assimilated Jewish family. The father owned a small shoe shop; the mother gave piano lessons; the family was modestly cultured rather than wealthy. He had been largely self-taught as a composer — the only formal instruction had come from Alexander von Zemlinsky, six years older than Schoenberg, who was the brother of his eventual first wife Mathilde. By his early twenties he had completed *Verklärte Nacht* and was beginning the work that would lead to the atonal revolution.

In March 1898, at twenty-three, he was baptized Lutheran at the Dorotheergasse Evangelical Church in Vienna. The decision was made for the standard reasons of the Viennese Jewish bourgeoisie of the period: to be a German composer, to be received in the German cultural establishment, to be free of the formal Jewish identity that the Habsburg empire still enforced through certain civic and professional restrictions. Zemlinsky was a witness. Mathilde, who was also Jewish and would be baptized to marry him in 1901, supported the decision. The baptism, like Heine's seventy-three years earlier, was a transactional act.

He spent the next quarter-century composing some of the most consequential music of the twentieth century. *Pelleas und Melisande*. *Gurre-Lieder*. The *Three Piano Pieces* op. 11 of 1909 that broke the tonal system. *Erwartung*. *Pierrot lunaire*. The development of the twelve-tone method between 1921 and 1923. The *Suite* op. 25, the first major twelve-tone work. The *Variations for Orchestra* op. 31. He had been at the center of European musical modernism. He had been, by the early 1920s, the most influential composer of his generation.

The 1923 letter to Kandinsky was the interior turning point. Schoenberg had been a friend and admirer of the Russian painter for fifteen years; they had corresponded extensively about the modernist project across painting and music. Schoenberg had heard, in the spring of 1923, that Kandinsky in Weimar had said certain things about Jews. Schoenberg wrote to him directly: *I have at last learnt the lesson that has been forced upon me during this year, and I shall never forget it. That I am no German, no European, indeed perhaps scarcely a human being (at least, the*

Europeans prefer the worst of their race to me), but that I am a Jew. The friendship ended. The letter was the document of Schoenberg's interior return to Jewish identity.

Over the next ten years the interior return became increasingly explicit in his work. The play *Der biblische Weg — The Biblical Way* — written 1925-1927, was a Zionist drama. *Moses und Aron*, begun in 1930, was the great Old Testament opera in which the Mosaic monotheism — strict, unrepresentable, true — is set against the Aaronic willingness to communicate the truth through the falsified imagery of the Golden Calf. The opera was unfinishable in a sense that mattered: Schoenberg never completed the third act because the philosophical and religious problem the opera was setting could not, by the music's own terms, be resolved.

In 1925 he had been appointed to head the master class in composition at the Prussian Academy of Arts in Berlin. He had moved to Berlin with his second wife Gertrud Kolisch, whom he had married in 1924 after the death of Mathilde the year before. He had taught some of the most important composers of the next generation. He had been at the height of his European career.

{

• • •

}

Hitler became Chancellor of Germany on January 30, 1933. The Reichstag fire was February 27. The Enabling Act was March 23. By April the Nazi regime was issuing the racial laws that would govern Jewish life in Germany for the next twelve years.

On May 17, 1933, the Prussian Academy of Arts dismissed Schoenberg from his professorship. The official reason given was the new racial law restricting Jews from holding civil-service positions. Schoenberg was, by the formal Lutheran baptism of 1898, not technically a Jew under the church-religion test the older Habsburg empire had used. He was, by the Nuremberg-style racial test that the Nazi state was beginning to apply, a Jew. The Lutheran certificate of 1898 was no longer relevant.

He left Berlin within days of the dismissal. He took Gertrud and their three-year-old daughter Nuria; he took whatever manuscripts and books he could pack; he traveled to Paris. He arrived at the end of May and rented an apartment in the Boulevard Lannes in the sixteenth arrondissement.

He was in Paris for six weeks before the ceremony of July 24. He had been thinking about the formal return to Judaism for years; he had been thinking about it more concretely since the appointment of Hitler in January; he had decided, when he arrived in Paris in May, that he would make the return formal at the next available opportunity. The opportunity was the Liberal Synagogue at 24 rue Copernic, where Rabbi Louis-Germain Lévy was prepared to receive him.

{

• • •

}

The Union Libérale Israélite at 24 rue Copernic was a Liberal — Reform — synagogue in the sixteenth arrondissement, a few blocks from where Schoenberg was staying. The synagogue had been founded in 1907; the building dated from 1908. It was one of the major Reform synagogues in Paris. Rabbi Louis-Germain Lévy, then in his early sixties, was the senior rabbi.

Schoenberg arrived at the synagogue on the late afternoon of Monday, July 24. He had asked Marc Chagall, the Russian-Jewish painter who had been living in Paris for several years, to act as one witness. Chagall had agreed. The other witness was Dmitri Marianoff, the writer and journalist who had married Albert Einstein's daughter Margot, and who was also in Paris. Schoenberg knew Marianoff slightly through musical and literary circles. The witnesses were both unsalaried; both had agreed to come simply because they were friends willing to be present at this kind of ceremony.

The ceremony itself was brief. There is no liturgy of return analogous to a baptism — Judaism does not have a formal sacrament for return; the rabbi accepted the petitioner's declaration of intent to live as a Jew, and the petitioner signed a document affirming the return. Schoenberg's document survives. It was prepared by Lévy's office; Schoenberg signed it; Chagall signed as witness; Marianoff signed as witness; Lévy signed as the rabbi.

Schoenberg added to the document a brief written statement of his own. The statement noted that the formal return that day was the public ratification of an interior return that had been decided long before — he cited his own works, including the unfinished *Moses und Aron* that he had been composing for three years, as evidence of the prior decision. He did not present the ceremony as the moment of his becoming a Jew. He presented it as the moment of his publicly being recognized as the Jew he had been for at least a decade.

When he had signed and the others had signed, the four men stood in the office briefly. Lévy offered a few words of welcome and a brief Hebrew blessing — the *shehecheyanu*, the prayer of thanksgiving for arriving at this moment. Schoenberg responded with the standard Hebrew *Amen* — a Hebrew word he had been hearing in his own *Moses und Aron* for several years now and that he was glad to be able to say in the office of a synagogue without irony.

Schoenberg, Chagall, and Marianoff left the synagogue together. They walked to a small café on the rue de la Pompe and had coffee. Chagall, who was the more sociable of the two witnesses, told Schoenberg about a painting he was working on. Marianoff said little. Schoenberg said he was glad it was done and that he could now consider the question settled.

{

• • •

}

Schoenberg and his family left Paris in October 1933. He had received an invitation from the Malkin Conservatory in Boston, which he accepted because no European country had offered a permanent academic position. He arrived in New York on October 31, 1933. He spent the academic year 1933-34 in Boston. The American climate was hard on his health; the Boston winter was particularly hard. In 1934 he moved to Los Angeles, accepting a position at the University of Southern California and then, from 1936, at UCLA, where he taught for the rest of his life.

The Los Angeles years brought him into the German exile community on the West Coast — Thomas Mann a few miles away in Pacific Palisades, Bruno Walter conducting in Los Angeles, Lion Feuchtwanger in Santa Monica, Bertolt Brecht through the war years, Theodor Adorno at the Institute for Social Research in exile. The community was Schoenberg's daily intellectual world from 1934 onward.

The American years produced two of the major works that defined his return to Judaism in musical terms. The *Kol Nidre* op. 39, composed in 1938 on commission from Rabbi Jakob Sonderling for Yom Kippur services in Los Angeles, was a setting of the Aramaic prayer that opens Yom Kippur. Schoenberg revised the traditional text — he wrote new English material for the opening — to emphasize what he understood as the universal moral content of the Day of Atonement, and he set the result for cantor, mixed chorus, and chamber orchestra. The work is the most explicit musical statement of his Jewish identity in the post-1933 years.

A Survivor from Warsaw op. 46, composed in 1947, is the seven-minute work for narrator, men's chorus, and orchestra in which a survivor of the Warsaw Ghetto describes the rounding-up of Jews and their forced singing of the *Shema Yisrael* before they are taken to be killed. The chorus enters with the *Shema* in Hebrew at the climax. The work is one of the most concentrated artistic responses to the Holocaust in twentieth-century music.

The relationship with Mann produced the most painful episode of his American years. Mann published *Doktor Faustus* in 1947 — the novel of the German composer Adrian Leverkühn whose Faustian pact with the devil is enacted partly through his mastery of a twelve-tone compositional method. Mann, working with Adorno's musical advice, had described the method in considerable technical detail, drawing directly on Schoenberg's actual procedures. He had not, in the first edition, credited Schoenberg as its originator. Schoenberg discovered the omission in 1948. He wrote to Mann directly, pointing out that the twelve-tone method described in the novel was his own invention and that Mann had attributed it, by implication, to a fictional composer who had ended his career in syphilitic madness and a pact with the devil. The correspondence across 1948 is among the most painful documents of the émigré culture of the period: an old composer, increasingly ill, defending his life's work against a great novelist who had, in good faith but with insufficient care, taken what was his without saying so. Mann eventually added an acknowledgment to subsequent editions — an *Author's Note* placing the twelve-tone method as Schoenberg's intellectual property. Schoenberg accepted the acknowledgment but never fully forgave Mann the original omission. The friendship, such as it had been, was diminished.

He continued *Moses und Aron* but never finished the third act. Acts I and II had been completed by 1933, before the move to Paris and America. Act III remained as a libretto without music; Schoenberg returned to it many times in the late 1940s but could not complete it. The opera as it stands is one of the great unfinished works of twentieth-century opera, and the unfinishability is, in some readings, part of its meaning.

He died in Los Angeles on July 13, 1951, at seventy-six. The day was Friday the thirteenth, which Schoenberg had feared and worked around throughout his life. He was buried in Los Angeles; his ashes were eventually returned to Vienna in 1974 and reinterred at the Vienna Central Cemetery alongside the other major Viennese composers.

{

• • •

}

Daniel sets the manuscript aside. The Schoenberg chapter has been the chapter of the return — the second of the un-conversions in the book, paired with Rosenzweig of twenty years before, but distinct from Rosenzweig in that Schoenberg had crossed first.

What strikes Daniel about Schoenberg is the doubled structure. The 1898 Lutheran baptism had been the Heine pattern in its standard form — the assimilation conversion of the educated Viennese Jew who wanted a German cultural career and who was still living, in 1898, in the world Heine had inhabited in 1825. The 1933 return was not the un-conversion of a man who had never converted; it was the second conversion of a man who had converted once and now converted back. The chapter is therefore in dialogue with both Heine (the original assimilation) and Rosenzweig (the refusal to follow the Heine pattern). Schoenberg had followed it. Then history had refused to ratify the following.

Daniel notes also, with the comparative attention these chapters have been demanding, that Schoenberg is one of the major figures of the great emigration of European Jewish and Jewish-adjacent intellectual culture from Nazi Germany and Austria. The list of those who left in the same years — Einstein, Mann, Brecht, Adorno, Horkheimer, Wigner, von Neumann, Hannah Arendt, Walter Benjamin (who did not survive the attempt), Stefan Zweig (who survived the journey but not the destination), Bruno Walter, Korngold, Eisler, Weill, the Vienna Circle scientists, the Frankfurt School in its entirety — is the list of the people Germany lost when it changed the terms of its civic contract in 1933. The cultural and scientific life of central Europe was, by 1939, transferred in significant measure to America, to England, and in smaller part to Palestine. Germany was, after the war, unable to fully recover what it had expelled. Many who left did not return; many who tried to return found that the country had not, even after 1945, become the country they had left. Schoenberg never returned. He lived the last seventeen years of his life in Los Angeles. The Vienna Central Cemetery received only his ashes, twenty-three years after his death. The story Daniel has been living near, indirectly, his whole adult life — many of his New York intellectual friends are descendants of émigrés from this period, and several of his teachers at Yale were the actual émigrés themselves — is one chapter in this larger story of what Germany lost when it decided that the Lutheran *Entréebillet* of 1898 was no longer honorable.

What Daniel notes also, with the small comparative attention of these chapters, is that the 1898 Lutheran baptism would not have saved Schoenberg from the Nuremberg laws of 1935 even if he had not formally returned in 1933. The racial test that the Nazi state was developing in the early 1930s explicitly overrode the church-religion test of the older empires. Heine's *Entréebillet* of 1825 had been honored, in legal terms, by the Prussian state for the rest of Heine's life. Schoenberg's *Entréebillet* of 1898 was withdrawn by the German state in 1935, retroactively, on grounds that had not existed when the ticket was issued. The figure of the modern transactional convert that Heine had inaugurated was, by the time of Schoenberg, a figure to whom the contract was no longer binding from the other party's side. The state had changed the terms.

The return was therefore, for Schoenberg, both more and less than for Rosenzweig. Less, because Rosenzweig had never converted, had never been complicit in the assimilation, had stood on the threshold and turned around. More, because Schoenberg had to undo a thirty-five-year prior commitment, had to acknowledge that the youthful baptism had been a mistake, had to recognize that the assimilation he had purchased with the 1898 ceremony had not been deliverable in the world that 1933 produced. He returned. He returned with the full weight of someone who had to undo as well as redo.

He closes the notebook. He goes to the listening chair. He chooses, this evening, Schoenberg's *Kol Nidre* op. 39 of 1938, in the recording by Pierre Boulez with the Ensemble InterContemporain and the BBC Singers. The work begins with the *Bell* — the orchestral signal — and the cantor's first invocation, in Schoenberg's revised English, of the Day of Atonement. The *Kol Nidre* prayer, the Aramaic formula of release from vows, follows. It is the prayer Rosenzweig had heard for the first time at the Berlin synagogue on the evening of October 10, 1913. It is the prayer Schoenberg, twenty-five years later, set as his musical declaration that he had returned.

Figures at the Threshold

Stein

Daniel sits at the desk. The Stein materials are out: *Endliches und Ewiges Sein* (Finite and Eternal Being); *Zum Problem der Einfühlung* (the doctoral dissertation on empathy); *Kreuzeswissenschaft* (The Science of the Cross); the autobiography *Aus dem Leben einer jüdischen Familie* (Life in a Jewish Family); the collected letters in the Carmelite Studies edition; the biographies by Waltraud Herbstrith and Sarah Borden; the volumes of philosophical correspondence with Roman Ingarden; the Carmelite documents.

Stein is the chapter the book has been preparing for and avoiding. She is the figure whose case combines, in the most painful possible way, every thread the chapters have been following: the German-Jewish assimilation tradition (she came from an observant Jewish family in Breslau and broke with the faith as a teenager); the high-philosophical training of the Husserl school (she was Husserl's research assistant at Göttingen and later Freiburg, completed her doctorate under him in 1916, was one of the most brilliant of his Göttingen students); the Catholic conversion (she was baptized at thirty in January 1922, after a single night in the summer of 1921 with Saint Teresa of Ávila's autobiography); the entrance into religious life (she became a Discalced Carmelite at Cologne in 1933, taking the name Teresa Benedicta of the Cross); and the Holocaust (she was arrested in the Netherlands in August 1942, transported to Auschwitz, and killed in the gas chamber on August 9, 1942 at the age of fifty).

The chapter must hold all of these threads at once. It cannot tell only the story of the 1922 baptism, because the 1942 deportation is what the 1922 baptism did not prevent and, in some readings, produced. It cannot tell only the story of Auschwitz, because the philosophical and spiritual life that led her to the Carmel of Echt in the late 1930s is the substance the chapter is honoring. It must hold both — the New Year's Day in Bergzabern when a thirty-year-old Husserl student became a Catholic, and the August morning at Auschwitz when a fifty-year-old Carmelite nun was killed for being a Jew.

He writes the dates at the top of the page: *1 January 1922 / 9 August 1942.*

{

• • •

}

She had been born in Breslau on October 12, 1891 — the youngest of eleven children, of whom seven survived childhood, in an observant Jewish family. Her father Siegfried Stein died when she was two; her mother Auguste — a woman of formidable practical and religious force — ran the family lumber business and raised the children alone. The household was Orthodox in observance. The major Jewish holidays were kept. The mother's Hebrew was good. The household read the Psalms.

Edith was, by her own later testimony, a precociously religious child until adolescence. At fourteen or fifteen she lost her childhood faith and declared herself an atheist. The break with her mother's Judaism was, in her teenage years, complete; she did not return to observance; she did not, in the years that followed, think much about religion in any positive sense.

She studied at Breslau, then transferred to Göttingen in 1913 to study philosophy with Edmund Husserl, who had founded the phenomenological school at Göttingen and whose seminars were the most demanding philosophical training in Germany. She was twenty-one. She had read Husserl's *Logical Investigations* and decided that this was the philosophy that mattered. Husserl accepted her as a student. Within two years she was one of the most brilliant of his Göttingen circle — Adolf Reinach, Hedwig Conrad-Martius, Roman Ingarden, Hans Lipps, the others were her company, and she was their intellectual peer.

In 1915 she interrupted her studies to volunteer as a Red Cross nurse during the First World War. She served in an infectious-diseases hospital at Mährisch-Weisskirchen in Moravia, treating Austrian soldiers with cholera, typhus, and dysentery. She returned to Freiburg in 1916 to complete her doctorate under Husserl, who had moved there from Göttingen. The dissertation — *Zum Problem der Einfühlung*, on the problem of empathy — was completed in 1916 and accepted *summa cum laude*. She remained as Husserl's research assistant until 1918.

She was, by 1920, a brilliant philosopher with no academic position. The German universities did not appoint women to professorships. Husserl himself had supported her *Habilitation* — the second doctorate that qualified candidates for university chairs — but no faculty would accept her thesis. She continued to write, to translate, to think. She was twenty-eight, single, brilliant, and at a loss.

{

• • •

}

In the summer of 1921 she went to visit friends — the philosopher Hedwig Conrad-Martius and her husband Theodor Conrad, both former Husserl students, both recent Protestant converts — at their country house at Bad Bergzabern in the Palatinate. The house was a converted farmhouse with a small vineyard. Edith stayed for several weeks. The Conrads were away on a brief journey one evening; Edith was alone in the house.

She had not been thinking about religion in any sustained sense. She had read Augustine in her doctoral years and had been moved without being changed. She had known Catholic and Protestant friends in the phenomenological circle who had begun to convert — Adolf Reinach, who had died at Verdun in 1917, had made a deathbed Christian commitment that had moved Stein when she heard about it; the Conrad-Martiuses had become Protestant; others were on similar paths. She had registered all this without acting on it.

That evening, alone in the house, she went to the Conrads' bookshelf and took down a book at random. The book was the autobiography of Saint Teresa of Ávila — *El Libro de la Vida,* in a German translation. Stein began to read.

She read through the night. The autobiography is a long, dense, idiosyncratic Spanish text from the 1560s, written by a Carmelite nun who was also one of the great mystics of the Catholic tradition and one of the great prose stylists of Spanish. Teresa describes her own life, her early religious formation, the years of mediocre observance, the breakthrough into mystical prayer, the founding of the Discalced Carmelite reform, the visions, the practical and spiritual work of a major religious order. Stein read it as a philosopher reads any serious text — slowly, carefully, with the trained Husserlian attention she had developed at Göttingen and Freiburg.

By morning she had decided she was a Catholic. The decision was not a decision in the ordinary sense. She had read the book; the book had described a structure of spiritual reality that Stein had recognized; the recognition was complete by the time the sun came up. She closed the book. She said, in the formula that has become the standard biographical one — and the formula is as plain as the moment was — *This is the truth.*

She bought a Catholic catechism the next day. She began the formal preparation for baptism. She wrote to her mother, in Breslau, about what she had decided. The mother's reaction was the most painful event of Edith's life until the events of 1942. Auguste Stein wept; she did not understand; she could not accept the decision; the relationship between mother and daughter would never quite recover.

{

• • •

}

The baptism was set for New Year's Day 1922 — January 1, the feast of the Circumcision in the older Catholic calendar, the day on which the eight-day-old Jewish infant Jesus had been received into the covenant of his people. The choice of date was Stein's own; she had wanted the symbolic resonance, the recognition that her entry into Christianity was, for her, an entry that did not require the rejection of her Jewish origin.

The ceremony was at the parish church of Saint Martin in Bergzabern. The pastor, Eugen Breitling, performed the baptism. Stein took the names *Theresia Hedwig* — Teresa for the saint who had brought her to faith, Hedwig for her sister, who had also recently become Catholic. The witnesses included Hedwig Conrad-Martius. The ceremony was brief. Stein was thirty.

The years that followed — 1922 to 1933 — were the years of her Catholic intellectual life. She moved to Speyer to teach at the Dominican girls' school of Saint Magdalena, where she would teach German for eight years. She continued her philosophical writing. She translated Saint Thomas Aquinas's *De Veritate — On Truth* — into German, the first major modern translation, completed in 1931. She lectured widely on Catholic education and on what she called the *philosophy of the woman,* addressing the new Catholic women's movement. She corresponded with Erich Przywara, the Jesuit philosopher of analogy. By the late 1920s she was one of the most significant philosophical voices in German Catholic thought.

She had been, since 1928, considering entrance into the Discalced Carmelites — Saint Teresa's order. She had postponed the decision out of consideration for her mother. By 1933 the postponement was no longer possible. The Nazi regime had come to power in January; the racial laws of April made it impossible for Stein, as a Jew under the new definition, to continue teaching at the Dominican school. She was dismissed in the spring. She wrote to Pope Pius XI asking him to issue an encyclical condemning Nazi antisemitism. The letter was not answered. The encyclical was not issued. She decided to enter Carmel.

She entered the Carmel of Cologne on October 14, 1933, six months after losing her teaching position. She took the name Sister Teresa Benedicta of the Cross — Teresa Blessed by the Cross. She made her first profession in 1935 and her final profession in 1938. The Carmel of Cologne, like all Carmels, was an enclosed contemplative community; the day was the seven offices, the work, the silence, the small interior life of a Discalced house. She continued to write — *Endliches und Ewiges Sein, Finite and Eternal Being*, the major philosophical work of her Carmelite years, was completed in 1937 — but the writing was now part of a contemplative life rather than a public academic one.

{

• • •

}

After the November 1938 Kristallnacht pogrom, the prioress of the Cologne Carmel decided that Stein and her sister Rosa — who had also converted to Catholicism and was attached to the convent as a *Tertiary* — were no longer safe in Germany. On the night of December 31, 1938, exactly seventeen years after Stein's baptism, the two sisters were smuggled across the border into the Netherlands. They were received at the Carmel of Echt in Limburg.

Stein continued her work at Echt. She completed *Kreuzeswissenschaft — The Science of the Cross* — her great study of Saint John of the Cross, her sister Carmelite of the sixteenth-century Spanish reform. She wrote letters. She had been writing, for some years, on the theme of the cross as the heart of the spiritual life — the participation in the suffering of Christ as the deepest form of Christian existence. The theme had been theoretical when she had begun. By 1940 it was no longer theoretical.

In May 1940, Nazi Germany invaded the Netherlands. The German occupation began. The deportations of Dutch Jews to the death camps in the East began in 1941 and accelerated through 1942.

On July 26, 1942, the Dutch Catholic bishops issued a pastoral letter, read in all Catholic churches in the Netherlands the following Sunday, formally condemning Nazi antisemitism and the deportations. The Reichskommissar in occupied Holland, Arthur Seyss-Inquart, retaliated. He ordered the immediate arrest of all Catholic Jews in the Netherlands — the Catholic-Jewish converts that the previous months had largely been spared.

On August 2, 1942, the SS came to the Carmel of Echt. They arrested Sister Teresa Benedicta of the Cross and her sister Rosa. Stein had been writing in her cell. She closed the manuscript. She put on her habit. She and Rosa walked out of the Carmel together. According to the testimony of those who saw them — testimony preserved in Carmelite documents and in survivors' accounts — Edith said to Rosa, in Dutch, *Komm, wir gehen für unser Volk.* Come, let us go for our people. The *our people* was the Jewish people. The Carmelite nun walking to her death recognized herself, at the moment of recognition, as a Jew going with her people.

The sisters were taken to Westerbork transit camp. They were held there for several days. Witnesses at Westerbork later remembered Sister Teresa Benedicta moving among the women and children, helping the mothers care for the children, praying. On August 7, 1942, they were loaded onto a transport to Auschwitz.

They arrived at Auschwitz-Birkenau on the morning of August 9, 1942. The transport was sent directly to the gas chambers on arrival. Edith Stein was killed that morning. She was fifty.

{

• • •

}

The cause for her canonization began within the Discalced Carmelite Order in the 1950s. She was declared a martyr by the Church — a person killed *in odium fidei,* in hatred of the faith — though the Catholic-Jewish complications of her case made the declaration controversial in some quarters. Pope John Paul II beatified her at Cologne on May 1, 1987. He canonized her, as Saint Teresa Benedicta of the Cross, on October 11, 1998. In 1999 he declared her one of the co-patronesses of Europe, alongside Bridget of Sweden and Catherine of Siena.

The canonization remains, in the Jewish-Christian dialogue of the late twentieth and early twenty-first centuries, contested. Some Jewish commentators have asked whether the Church can canonize as a Catholic martyr a woman who was killed because she was a Jew, regardless of her own conversion — whether the formal recognition of Stein's sanctity is, in some sense, a re-appropriation of her by the Church that had not done enough to save her. Others have noted that Stein's own statement at Echt — *Come, let us go for our people* — claimed her Jewish identity even at the moment of her Carmelite martyrdom, and that the canonization can be read as honoring this claim. The question is not formally resolved.

{

• • •

}

Daniel sets the manuscript aside. The Stein chapter has been the chapter of the conversion that did not save. The 1922 baptism took her into the Catholic Church. The Catholic Church did not save her from the gas chamber. The 1942 deportation was, in fact, accelerated by the Dutch bishops' letter — the very Catholic gesture of solidarity with the Jews that Stein and her co-religionists had been hoping the Catholic Church would make for years brought down on her, when it finally came, the retaliation that killed her.

What strikes Daniel about the Stein case is the layering. She was a Jew who became a Catholic; she was a Catholic who recognized at the moment of her death that she was going as a Jew; she was a Carmelite nun who had been writing on the cross as the heart of the spiritual life when the SS came for her. None of these is reducible to the others. Each is, in its own register, true.

The chapter makes Daniel think about the way the conversions in the book have not, finally, been about the simple movement of a person from one tradition to another. They have been about the way a person who has converted continues to carry the tradition they came from inside the tradition they have entered. Heine remained, in the *Mattratzengruft*, a Jewish poet writing under a Christian name. Mendelssohn produced the great Lutheran sacred work of his century while keeping the *Phaedon* of his Jewish grandfather on the second shelf of the breakfast room. Schoenberg returned to Judaism with the German musical training that had been the gift of his Lutheran years. Stein went to her death as a Carmelite nun saying to her sister, in Dutch, *Come, let us go for our people.*

The conversion is therefore not a substitution but an addition, and the addition is unstable, and the instability is, in some sense, the truth of the conversion. Stein's case is the limit case because the addition was paid for, in her case, with the life. She was killed for a Judaism she had formally left and a Catholicism that did not protect her. She has been canonized for the Catholicism that did not protect her, on grounds that include the Judaism she had formally left. The whole figure exists in a kind of permanent unresolved doubleness that is, perhaps, the only honest way to be a Jewish Catholic in the twentieth century.

What Daniel finds himself returning to, when he closes the chapter, is Stein's earliest philosophical work — the doctoral dissertation of 1916 on the problem of empathy. *Zum Problem der Einfühlung* is the work in which the twenty-five-year-old Husserl student worked out, with the rigor of the Göttingen phenomenological method, the structure of how one human consciousness comes to know and partially inhabit the experience of another. Empathy, in Stein's careful formulation, is not sympathy — which is a feeling of pity directed at another from outside — but the act by which one consciousness reaches into another and partially shares what is being experienced there. The dissertation distinguishes individual empathy, directed at one other person, from a collective empathy in which one shares the experience of a group.

Daniel notes, with the small honesty these chapters have been demanding, that empathy in Stein's sense is the moral center of his private life. He has been an empathetic man for as long as he can remember. The trait came, he thinks, from his Mexican childhood — from the kind, mostly poorly-educated maids and household helpers who had cared for him in the years his mother was occupied with the family business, and with whom he had bonded the way children bond with the people who feed and clean for them. He was capable, from very young, of feeling what they felt; he was angered, sometimes disproportionately, when they were offended or treated badly by anyone in the household. The trait persisted. It has organized, more than he would have said in any prior chapter of his life, the moral structure of his attentions: he has been particularly responsive to women in difficult situations — exploited, mistreated, disappointed — and he has noticed suffering in his immediate surroundings with a clarity he has not always been able to explain.

He thinks of the woman on his floor. Beacon Court has four apartments per floor and four elevators; one rarely encounters neighbors except in the lobby. There is a woman in her early forties on his floor who always greets him in passing — *Good morning, Mr. Ferrara. Good evening, Mr. Ferrara.* She has, he gathers, some minor mental difficulty; she lives alone; she does not seem to have visitors. Her loneliness has saddened him for some time. He has not invited her for coffee. He does not plan to. The Stein chapter has made him aware, however, that the small daily empathy he feels for her, and has been feeling without naming, is part of the moral fabric the rest of his life is organized around.

The empathy is local. It is for the people he can see. He is honest enough to acknowledge that his empathy for distant suffering — the populations of conflicts in countries he cannot picture, the abstract victims of forces he does not directly observe — is weaker, more occasional, more easily set down. Stein's empathy, by 1942, had been collective and total; she had recognized at Echt that she was going as a Jew with her people, and the *people* in question included Jews she had never met. Daniel's empathy has not been collective in that sense. It has been the small everyday attention to particular others — the maid, the doorman, the woman on the floor — and he has not pretended otherwise.

He closes the notebook. He goes to the listening chair. He chooses, this evening, Poulenc's *Dialogues of the Carmelites* — the 1956 opera on the Carmelite martyrs of Compiègne, sixteen Discalced Carmelite nuns guillotined in Paris on July 17, 1794, during the Terror. The closing scene of the opera is one of the most extraordinary in twentieth-century music: the nuns walk to the guillotine singing the *Salve Regina,* and the chorus is reduced one voice at a time as each sister is killed, until only the last voice remains. The recording is the older Pierre Dervaux conducting at the Paris Opéra. Daniel listens. The *Salve Regina* begins.

Figures at the Threshold

Weil

Daniel sits at the desk. The Weil materials are out: the *Cahiers* in the four-volume Plon edition; *La Pesanteur et la grâce* (*Gravity and Grace*); *L'Enracinement* (*The Need for Roots*); *Attente de Dieu* (*Waiting for God*), the letters to Father Joseph-Marie Perrin in which she explained her refusal of baptism; the *Œuvres complètes* in the Gallimard edition; the McLellan biography; the more recent biography by Robert Zaretsky. Beside them, a small parallel set of materials: Walter Benjamin's *Illuminations* in the Hannah Arendt-edited Schocken volume; the Belknap *Selected Writings* in four volumes; the Eiland and Jennings biography; the small volume of letters to Gershom Scholem.

The Weil chapter is, for Daniel, the chapter closest to his own stated ambivalence. She is the figure who heard the call — clearly, in 1938 at the Abbey of Solesmes during Holy Week — and who nevertheless refused, until her death five years later, to be baptized. She is the patron, if a saint can be patron of such a thing, of the unbaptized seeker. Daniel had said, half as a joke, in the conversation with Ingrid in the courtyard fifteen months ago, that if he were ever called he could try to emulate Simone Weil. Ingrid had said it was not really a joke. The chapter is the test of how much of a joke it was.

He has decided to bring with him, in this chapter, a figure who has been waiting in the corner of the book for a long time without quite finding a place: Walter Benjamin. Benjamin was Weil's contemporary — born 1892, killed by his own hand at the Spanish-French border at Portbou on September 26, 1940, three years before Weil's death at Ashford. Benjamin was the secular Jewish intellectual whose entire life had been lived at the edge of the religious question without ever crossing to it; Weil was the secular Jewish intellectual who had crossed almost all the way and refused, at the last threshold, to step over. Together, the two figures bracket the kind of position Daniel himself occupies — present to the religious question, attentive to it, not converting from it. The chapter belongs to Weil. Benjamin will appear at the end, in the frame close, as the shadow companion the chapter has been carrying.

He writes the dates at the top of the page: *Solesmes 1938 / Ashford 1943 / Portbou 1940.*

{

• • •

}

She had been born in Paris on February 3, 1909, into a Jewish family that was, in the standard French phrase of the period, *israélite* — assimilated, secular, well-educated, comfortable. Her father Bernard was a doctor; her mother Selma a cultured woman with strong opinions; her older brother André would become one of the great mathematicians of the twentieth century, a founder of the Bourbaki group. The household kept no Jewish observance.

The children were not given any positive Jewish formation; they grew up with the diffuse French secular humanism of the cultivated republican bourgeoisie of the early Third Republic.

She studied at the Lycée Henri-IV under Alain — Émile Chartier — the famous lay philosopher whose influence on French intellectual life of the period was enormous. She entered the École Normale Supérieure in 1928 and passed the *agrégation* in philosophy in 1931, third in her class; Simone de Beauvoir was first. The two famous Simones of the interwar Sorbonne knew each other formally without becoming friends.

Weil taught philosophy at provincial *lycées* — Le Puy, Auxerre, Roanne, Bourges, Saint-Quentin — through the 1930s. She was a difficult colleague; she was repeatedly transferred for political reasons. She had become, by the early 1930s, a serious left-wing political activist — close to but never inside the French Communist Party, which she considered already corrupted by Stalinism. In 1934-35 she took a year of unpaid leave from teaching to work in factories at Alsthom and Renault, in order to know the working-class life she had been writing about. The factory year produced what she would later call, with the precision the experience had given her, *malheur* — affliction — the specific condition of people whose dignity has been taken from them by the structure of the work they are forced to do.

In summer 1936 she went briefly to Spain to support the Republican side in the civil war, joining an anarchist column under Buenaventura Durruti. She burned her foot in a cooking accident within weeks; her parents came to retrieve her; she returned to France. The Spanish experience confirmed her conviction that political militancy of the kind she had been practicing was insufficient to address what was, beneath the political surface, a metaphysical condition.

{

• • •

}

The religious turn began in 1935. Three specific incidents — what Weil herself, in the autobiographical letter to Father Perrin written in 1942, called *contacts with Catholicism* — moved her from her earlier secular position toward a recognition she had not been seeking.

The first was at Póvoa de Varzim, a fishing village on the Portuguese coast, in summer 1935. On the eve of the patronal feast of the Virgin of Carmel she walked through the village and saw the fishermen's wives carrying candles around the boats in procession, singing ancient hymns of Mediterranean Catholic devotion. *I had the conviction, suddenly,* she wrote later to Perrin, *that Christianity is preeminently the religion of slaves, that slaves cannot help belonging to it, and I among the others.*

The second was at Assisi in 1937. Standing in the small chapel of Santa Maria degli Angeli — the chapel where Saint Francis had prayed in the early years of his religious life — *something stronger than I,* she wrote, *forced me, for the first time in my life, to my knees.* She was twenty-eight.

The third — the decisive contact — was at the Abbey of Solesmes during Holy Week 1938. Solesmes was the Benedictine monastery near the Loire that had since the nineteenth century been the center of the modern Gregorian chant revival. Weil attended every office from Palm Sunday through Easter Sunday. She was suffering from migraines so severe she could barely follow what was being sung; the music made the headaches worse rather than better, and yet she kept attending.

A young Englishman she met at Solesmes during the week — *a young Englishman of pure radiance*, in her later phrase — introduced her to the seventeenth-century English religious poetry of George Herbert. He recommended in particular the short lyric called *Love* (*III*). Weil took the poem with her. She memorized it. She had been in the habit, during the worst of the headaches, of reciting things to herself as a way of bearing the pain.

It was while reciting *Love* (*III*) to herself, in the period after Solesmes, that the moment Weil afterward described as the central experience of her life took place. She was reciting the poem when, *Christ himself came down and took possession of me.* The phrase is from the Perrin letter. The experience was, as far as Daniel can determine from her own descriptions, what the Catholic mystical tradition called an infused contemplation — a state in which the mystic does not produce or seek the experience but is given it. She had not been thinking about Christ. She had not, until that moment, considered herself a Christian in any sense. The experience took place without her consent and without her preparation. She accepted it as what it was. She did not look for it again.

{

• • •

}

Between 1938 and her death in 1943, Weil was in increasingly active engagement with Catholic thought and practice. She read the Greek Fathers in the original. She read Saint John of the Cross. She read the New Testament with the same close attention she had brought to Plato in her doctoral years. Her *Notebooks* of this period are one of the great records in twentieth-century thought of a non-Christian's serious engagement with Christian theology.

In 1941 she met Father Joseph-Marie Perrin, the Dominican priest at Marseille who would be her spiritual director for the rest of her life. Perrin was nearly blind — the result of a wartime injury — and his blindness gave the relationship a particular intensity; Weil read texts to him aloud. The correspondence between them from 1941 to 1943 is the single most important document of her religious thought. It includes the long letter she wrote to him in May 1942, before she left for America, in which she set out, with the precision of a philosopher, why she would not accept baptism.

The reasons she gave were several. She did not want to leave the great mass of unbelievers in which she felt she belonged; she felt called to remain *au seuil de l'Église* — at the threshold of the Church — *sans entrer*, without entering. She had reservations about specific Catholic doctrines — the *Anathema sit* of the councils, the historical violence the Church had committed in the name of unity — that she could not accept without intellectual dishonesty. She believed her vocation was precisely to be one of those who remained outside, who could speak to the unbelievers in their own language, who could carry the kernel of Christian truth across to people for whom the Church itself was a closed door. *I love God, Christ, and the Catholic faith as much as it is possible for so miserably inadequate a creature to love them. But Saint Thomas's anathemas weigh on me. I cannot be baptized.*

Perrin did not press her. He understood that her position was a position of integrity. He continued to be her director and friend until her death.

{

• • •

}

In May 1942 she left France for the United States with her parents. She lived briefly in New York, attended Catholic Mass without taking communion, and continued to write. In November 1942 she sailed to England to join the Free French in London. She worked at General de Gaulle's headquarters as an analyst and writer. She wrote *L'Enracinement* — *The Need for Roots* — the long essay on what would be required to rebuild France after the war, which became, after her death, the central text of her political thought.

She had refused, since her arrival in London, to eat more than the food rationed to civilians in occupied France. The reasoning was a moral solidarity that the Free French doctors who treated her described, with the technical precision the case required, as a kind of deliberate self-starvation. She had been tubercular since the previous spring; the inadequate eating accelerated the disease. By April 1943 she was hospitalized at the Middlesex Hospital in London. In August she was transferred to a sanatorium at Ashford in Kent.

She died at Ashford on August 24, 1943, of cardiac failure complicated by tuberculosis and malnutrition. She was thirty-four. The coroner's verdict was suicide by self-starvation, contested by those who had known her. She was buried in the New Cemetery at Ashford.

The publication of her work began almost immediately. *La Pesanteur et la grâce* appeared in 1947, edited by Gustave Thibon. *L'Enracinement* appeared in 1949. *Attente de Dieu* — the letters to

Perrin — appeared in 1950. By the late 1950s she was recognized as one of the major religious thinkers of the century. T. S. Eliot wrote the preface to the English translation of *The Need for Roots*. Albert Camus, who edited her work for Gallimard, considered her the only great spirit of the period.

{

• • •

}

The shadow figure who has been with the chapter from its opening. Walter Benjamin had been born in Berlin on July 15, 1892, into an assimilated Jewish family roughly comparable to the Weils' in Paris — comfortable, secular, cultivated. He had completed his doctorate in 1919 at Bern. He had failed, in 1925, to obtain the *Habilitation* at Frankfurt that would have qualified him for a university chair: the rejected thesis was *The Origin of German Tragic Drama*, now considered one of the major works of twentieth-century criticism.

He had spent the next fifteen years as a freelance critic, essayist, translator. He had translated Baudelaire and Proust into German. He had written *One-Way Street*, the *Arcades Project* (which he never completed), the great essay *The Work of Art in the Age of Mechanical Reproduction* of 1936, the *Theses on the Philosophy of History* of 1940. He had been close to Theodor Adorno, who had defended him to the Institute for Social Research and arranged the small stipend that kept him alive in Paris through the late 1930s. He had been close to Bertolt Brecht, who had argued the Marxist case to him. He had been close, longest of all, to Gershom Scholem, the great scholar of Jewish mysticism in Jerusalem, who had argued the Jewish case and had urged Benjamin for fifteen years to come to Palestine.

He had not converted. He had not, in the way Weil had, undergone any specific religious experience that asked him to convert. His thought had absorbed Jewish mystical materials — the Kabbalah, messianic theology, the Lurianic image of the broken vessels — and had absorbed Marxist materialism, and had absorbed the close reading of the modern poet (Baudelaire) and the modern photograph (the Atget studies), and had produced, in the unique alloy of his prose, a way of writing about the modern that was unlike any other. He had stood at the religious threshold throughout his life and had not crossed.

He had fled Paris in June 1940 ahead of the German occupation. He had joined the small group of refugees attempting to cross the Pyrenees into Spain in September. The group reached the Spanish border at Portbou on September 25. Spanish border guards refused them entry. They were told they would be returned to France the next day. Benjamin, who had been carrying a manuscript he believed was his most important work — the *Theses on the Philosophy of History*, which had not been published — and who could not face being returned to the German authorities, took an overdose of morphine that night at the small Hotel de Francia in Portbou. He died on September 26, 1940. The other members of the group were allowed to continue the next day; the Spanish authorities had reversed their decision overnight. The manuscript was never recovered. He was forty-eight.

{

• • •

}

Daniel sets the manuscript aside. The Weil-and-Benjamin chapter has been the chapter of the two Jewish intellectuals at the edge of the religious question — both formed by the secular Jewish bourgeoisie of pre-1914 Europe, both confronting in the interwar period the catastrophes the secular settlement of their parents could not absorb, both dying in their thirties or forties before the war's end, both casualties of the Nazi pressure that was the primary historical force of their adult lives. Benjamin died in Spain in 1940 by his own morphine; Weil died in Kent in 1943 by her refusal to eat more than the French ration. Neither survived to forty-five.

What strikes Daniel about the pair is the differential at the threshold. Weil had crossed almost everything except the formal sacrament. She had read more Christian theology than most Catholic priests; she had attended Mass for years; she had had the central mystical experience while reciting George Herbert; she had been director by Father Perrin since 1941; the only thing she had not done was the baptism itself. Benjamin had not done any of it. He had been, throughout his life, a secular Jewish intellectual whose interest in religious materials — Kabbalah, messianism, theology — was philosophical and historical rather than personal-religious. The Scholem letters of the 1920s and 1930s show Scholem urging him toward Judaism in Palestine; Benjamin always refused, gently. He had no equivalent of Weil's Solesmes moment. He had no Father Perrin. He had no recited *Love* (*III*).

What Daniel finds, when he holds the two figures side by side, is that he is closer to both of them than he is to most of the figures in the book. With Weil he shares — though in a much weaker register — the love of sacred music and of the great Catholic art and architecture; the long visits to the abbey churches of France and

Spain; the willingness to sit in the back of a Cistercian church for an hour during Vespers as a non-Catholic listening to chant. With Benjamin he shares — though again in a weaker register — the engagement with the modern, with film and photography and the changed ecology of attention that mass media has produced; the constitutional lawyer's interest in how images and information shape political life; the secular Jewish intellectual's relation to the religious materials of his ancestral tradition that he has not, finally, embraced.

He cannot, on examination, claim Weil's mysticism as his own. He has never had the Solesmes moment. He has never been *taken possession of by Christ.* The aesthetic engagement that has been the constant of his sixty years has not produced, in his case, an interior visitation. He has stood at the threshold without being asked to cross. He has stood there, more accurately, without anything having approached him from the other side. His version of Weil's position is the version Weil herself, at her most generous, would have made room for: the unbeliever who watches with attention, who respects the mystery, who does not pretend to understand it from inside, and who does not pretend, either, that the mystery is not there. Weil had refused baptism in order to remain *au seuil de l'Église*, at the threshold, on behalf of those for whom the threshold was where they belonged. Daniel has been at the threshold for a different reason — not in solidarity with the unbelievers but as one of them — but the geography is the same.

He closes the notebook. He goes to the listening chair. He chooses, this evening, the recording of Gregorian chant by the Choir of the Monks of the Abbey of Saint-Pierre de Solesmes — the abbey at which Weil had her central experience during Holy Week 1938. The selection is from the office for the days of Holy

Week. The voices begin: *Christus factus est pro nobis obediens usque ad mortem.* Christ became obedient for us unto death.

Figures at the Threshold

Greene and Waugh

Daniel sits at the desk. The Greene and Waugh materials are out: for Greene, *Brighton Rock, The Power and the Glory, The Heart of the Matter, The End of the Affair, The Quiet American*; the autobiography *A Sort of Life* and the second volume *Ways of Escape*; the Norman Sherry biography in three volumes; *The Lawless Roads* travel book of 1939. For Waugh, *Decline and Fall, A Handful of Dust, Brideshead Revisited*, the *Sword of Honour* trilogy, *Helena*; the diaries; the letters; Selina Hastings's biography; and — on a low shelf, in the green Chapman & Hall first edition of 1939, with the slight foxing of a book that had been somewhere damp at some point — *Robbery Under Law: The Mexican Object Lesson.* Daniel had bought it at the Strand on lower Broadway about thirty years ago, for two dollars, in the days when one could still find first editions of disavowed books in the back-room bins.

Greene and Waugh are the chapter the book has been pointing to since the Newman chapter. They are the great twentieth-century English Catholic novelists — Greene received in February 1926 at the cathedral of Saint Barnabas in Nottingham, Waugh received in September 1930 at the Farm Street Jesuit church in Mayfair.

Their conversions were canonical events in the small history of the English Catholic minority. Their novels — *The Power and the Glory*, *The End of the Affair*, *Brideshead Revisited*, the *Sword of Honour* trilogy — are among the major literary expressions of twentieth-century English-language Catholicism. Both are firmly in the canon.

The chapter, however, is not principally about the conversions or the canonical novels. It is about the dark passage in their joint Catholic biography that the standard reception has either glossed over or treated as a footnote: the entanglement, in the late 1930s, with the propaganda campaign that the British and American oil companies mounted against the Mexican government after the expropriation of March 1938. Both Waugh and Greene traveled to Mexico in this period. Both wrote books that attacked the Cárdenas regime. Waugh's book — *Robbery Under Law* — was openly funded by the Pearson/Cowdray interests, who had been among the major British investors in Mexican oil and whose holdings had been expropriated. Greene's trip was funded — less openly, more circuitously — by the Catholic Church-aligned networks that had been organizing the international protest against the Cárdenas regime's anticlerical laws and its land reform. Both writers, in this period, took money or its equivalent from interested parties to write books that those parties wanted written.

Daniel — Mexican by birth, with a particular claim on the country whose government these two great Catholic writers were paid to denounce — has come to the chapter with something more personal than the usual reader's interest. The chapter is the chapter of pragmatic, politically entangled Catholicism, set against the mystical conversions of Pascal and Claudel, the philosophical conversions of Newman and Stein, the un-conversions of Spinoza and Rosenzweig and Schoenberg. Greene and Waugh are the figures whose Catholicism, however sincere as personal faith, was for a moment in 1938 and 1939 the cover under which they were carrying water for interests that had nothing to do with the Catholic faith and everything to do with the corporate balance sheet.

He writes the dates at the top of the page: *Mexico, 1938 / The books, 1939–1940.*

{

• • •

}

Greene had converted in February 1926, at twenty-one. He had been a journalist on the *Nottingham Journal*; he had fallen in love with Vivien Dayrell-Browning, a serious convert who had told him she would not marry a non-Catholic; he had taken instruction with Father George Trollope, a former actor turned priest, at the cathedral of Saint Barnabas in Nottingham; he was received on February 26. The conversion was tied to the marriage. It was also more than the marriage. He had been moving toward Catholicism intellectually for some months before he met Vivien; he had been reading Newman, Belloc, Chesterton; he had concluded that the Catholic position on the existence of God was at least intellectually defensible, which was as much as he was willing to claim. He would, for the next sixty-five years, describe himself as a *Catholic agnostic* — a phrase that did the work of holding together his persistent religious doubt and his persistent Catholic practice.

Waugh had converted in September 1930, at twenty-six. The conversion came after the breakup of his first marriage to Evelyn

Gardner — *She-Evelyn* in the period's gossip — and the failure of his early literary period to settle into anything stable. He had taken instruction with Father Martin D'Arcy SJ, the brilliant Jesuit philosopher at Campion Hall, Oxford, who had been receiving educated converts at the Farm Street church for years. He was received on September 29, the feast of Saint Michael. The conversion, by Waugh's later account, had been a turning toward order and away from the disorder of his early adult life. He would, for the next thirty-six years, be the most public English Catholic novelist of his generation, the defender of the old Latin Mass against the reforms of Vatican II, the polemicist of a Catholicism more conservative than the contemporary English hierarchy was comfortable with.

Both became, in their own ways, deeply serious about the Catholic faith. Both became its great twentieth-century English novelists.

{

• • •

}

Mexico in the late 1930s was the focus of two major international controversies that the British and American Catholic right had been following with growing alarm for a decade.

The first was the religious situation, which the propaganda called a religious persecution and which the Mexican government treated as the constitutional disestablishment of the Catholic Church. The relationship between Church and state in Mexico had been complicated for nearly a century. The 1857 Constitution under President Benito Juárez had established Mexico as a secular state on a model comparable to the French

— civil marriage and civil birth certificates were the only legally recognized acts; religious baptisms and weddings continued to be celebrated and were never prohibited, but had no civil force; church property was nationalized; clerical privileges were abolished. The 1917 Constitution, in the wake of the Mexican Revolution, intensified these provisions. The Mexican model, like the French model after the 1905 separation, asserted public control over education and the public square and sought to limit the institutional power of the Church without forbidding private belief.

The Calles administration of the mid-1920s enforced these constitutional provisions more strictly than they had been enforced in decades. The Calles Law of 1926 imposed criminal penalties on the public exercise of clerical functions outside Church-registered premises. The Mexican episcopate, with Vatican backing, responded by suspending public worship across the country: from the summer of 1926 the bishops effectively closed the churches and framed the conflict in the international Catholic press as an attack on religious liberty. This decision — itself a Catholic action rather than a state imposition — radicalized lay Catholics, particularly in the central-western states, and contributed to the outbreak of the Cristero War of 1926-29. The war was an armed peasant rebellion in roughly half a dozen states — Jalisco, Michoacán, Guanajuato, Zacatecas, Colima, parts of Querétaro and Aguascalientes; it was not a national civil war, and most of Mexico continued ordinary life through the period. The war ended in the Modus Vivendi of 1929. But specific states — Tabasco, Veracruz, Sonora — continued to enforce harsh anticlerical laws into the 1930s. Tabasco under Tomás Garrido Canabal had become notorious; priests had been required to marry; church buildings had been seized; the cult of personality of the governor had replaced public Catholic practice.

The second was the oil nationalization. On March 18, 1938, after the Mexican Supreme Court had ruled in favor of striking oil workers and the foreign oil companies had refused to comply with the ruling, President Lázaro Cárdenas signed the decree expropriating the entire foreign-owned petroleum industry. Pemex was created. The American and British companies — Standard Oil of New Jersey, Royal Dutch Shell, the Pearson interests of Lord Cowdray, others — lost assets that had been valued in the hundreds of millions of dollars of the period. The companies launched, in response, a major international propaganda campaign — boycotts of Mexican oil, lobbying of foreign governments, sponsored journalism, sponsored books.

The two controversies reinforced each other in the propaganda. The argument made by the campaign — and made with considerable rhetorical effectiveness in the British and American Catholic press of 1938-1939 — was that the Cárdenas regime was simultaneously persecuting Catholics, expropriating private property, and aligning itself with the international communist movement. The argument was true in some of its parts and false in others, but the rhetorical package was effective. It produced the political climate in which Greene and Waugh, for different reasons and with different sponsorships, traveled to Mexico in 1938 to write books denouncing the regime.

{

• • •

}

Waugh's trip was the more straightforward of the two in its financing. The Pearson family — Lord Cowdray and his heirs, who had built the great British oil company in Mexico in the early twentieth century — retained substantial interests in Mexican oil at the time of the expropriation. The family approached Chapman & Hall in 1938 with a proposal: would they commission Waugh, who was by then their bestselling novelist and a serious Catholic, to travel to Mexico and write a book documenting what the Pearson interests considered the catastrophic consequences of the Cárdenas regime?

Waugh agreed. The fee, the expenses, the travel arrangements were handled discreetly. He sailed from England in August 1938 and spent eight weeks in Mexico — in Mexico City, in Tampico, in Cuernavaca, in Veracruz. He met with the British community, with Catholic clergy still operating in the more lenient states, with foreign journalists. He did not meet with anyone in the Cárdenas administration. He read what he had been given by the Pearson representatives. He returned to England in October.

Robbery Under Law: The Mexican Object Lesson was written in the winter of 1938-39 and published by Chapman & Hall in summer 1939. The book is a sustained polemic against the Cárdenas government. Waugh argued that the expropriation was an unjustified seizure of foreign property, that the Mexican government was effectively socialist in its sympathies and likely communist in its long-term direction, that the Catholic persecution was real and severe, and that the Mexican people — whom he treated, throughout the book, with a mixture of paternalism and contempt — were being misgoverned by a corrupt and ideologically driven regime. The book contained specific factual claims about Mexican government practices that ranged from accurate to contested to demonstrably false. It contained a great deal of

Waugh's characteristic Catholic-conservative invective. It was, in its own polemical register, a competent piece of work.

It was also, Waugh later understood, an embarrassment. He never reprinted it during his lifetime. He excluded it from the volumes of his collected work that he supervised. He referred to it, in private correspondence of the 1950s and 1960s, as a piece of journalism he had been paid to write and would not have written under his own initiative. He acknowledged, with the dry self-deprecation of his late style, that his Mexican expertise had been somewhat limited. The book has remained, in the standard accounts of Waugh's career, the embarrassed footnote — present in the bibliographies, absent from the canon.

The copy Daniel keeps on the low shelf is the green Chapman & Hall first edition of 1939. The book is, on Daniel's lawyer's reading, a sponsored pamphlet in book form — a polemic commissioned, paid for, and published to advance the specific commercial interests of the Pearson family, dressed in the conventions of the travel-essay and the political-journalistic survey. In its specific charges it is, in addition, intermittently libelous in the standard legal sense — against named Mexican officials, against the regime as such, against the Mexican character that the more sophisticated chapters tried to soften. The libel is the surface symptom; the sponsorship is the underlying nature of the work. Daniel keeps it as evidence. It is, on his shelf, the documentary remainder of what one of the great English Catholic novelists of the twentieth century was willing to write when he was paid by the right interests.

{

• • •

}

Greene's Mexican trip was earlier in 1938 and somewhat more circuitous in its sponsorship. The trip was, on the surface, undertaken on his own initiative — he had become interested in the persecution of Mexican Catholics through his coverage of the topic for the British Catholic press, and he had proposed the journey to his publishers and to several Catholic organizations. The financing was assembled from a combination of his publisher's advance, a stipend from Catholic-aligned sources, and travel arrangements that were facilitated by the Knights of Columbus and other American Catholic groups that had been organizing the international response to the Mexican religious situation. He met with American Catholic representatives in the United States both on his way down and on his way back; the meetings included briefings on the larger international campaign and discussions of how his eventual writing might serve it.

Greene traveled to Mexico in February-April 1938 — slightly before the oil expropriation of March, although the political climate had been building for some time. He went to Tabasco specifically — Garrido Canabal's state, where the most severe anti-Catholic measures had been in force, and where a clandestine Catholic priest was reported to be operating in the back country. He met with priests in hiding. He met with Catholic laity. He saw what Tabasco was, and the seeing was the basis of the book that would survive the trip.

The Lawless Roads — Greene's travel book of 1939 — emerged from the journey. The book is a hostile and sometimes contemptuous account of Mexico, of Mexicans, of the Cárdenas regime. It treats the religious persecution as the central fact of contemporary Mexican life. It contains, in its particular factual claims, less of Waugh's libel and more of Greene's specific reportorial accuracy — Greene had actually been to Tabasco, had actually met persecuted priests, had actually seen what he described. But it shares with Waugh's book the political shape: Mexico as a corrupt, anti-Catholic, quasi-communist regime that the Catholic and democratic West needed to oppose.

What separates Greene from Waugh in the Mexican episode is the novel that emerged. *The Power and the Glory*, published in 1940, was the great fiction Greene drew from the material. The novel — the *whisky priest* on the run from the regime in Tabasco, his moral struggle, his eventual capture and execution — is one of the major Catholic novels of the twentieth century. It transcends the polemical context of the travel book; it survives as literature in a way *The Lawless Roads* does not. Greene himself, in later years, considered *The Power and the Glory* his best novel. He was less embarrassed by the Mexican episode than Waugh was, partly because the novel had redeemed it.

But the novel had been written from the political-economic context Greene had been operating inside. The trip was paid in some part by the international Catholic-conservative campaign against Cárdenas. The travel book delivered what the campaign had been hoping for. The novel, while serious literature, took for granted the same political shape — the regime as predatory, the Catholic Mexican people as victims, the priest as the heroic remnant. The novel is great in spite of, not because of, the politics of its origins.

Daniel notes, with the small honesty these chapters have been demanding, that Greene's case is more complicated than Waugh's. *The Power and the Glory* is a major work; Daniel has read it three times across his life; it survives the political compromise of the trip in a way that *Robbery Under Law* cannot survive its compromise. But the trip itself, and the book that came directly from it, are part of the same dark chapter.

{

• • •

}

Both writers continued for decades after the Mexican episode. Greene wrote *The Heart of the Matter* in 1948, *The End of the Affair* in 1951, *The Quiet American* in 1955, *A Burnt-Out Case* in 1960, the late espionage and Catholic novels through the 1980s. He died in Vevey in 1991, at eighty-six.

Waugh wrote *Brideshead Revisited* in 1945 — the great Catholic novel of his career, the country-house meditation on grace and the inadequacy of the converts who came late to it. He wrote *Helena* in 1950, his preferred among his own books. He wrote the *Sword of Honour* trilogy across the 1950s. He died, after a long decline, on Easter Sunday 1966.

Both became firmly canonical English Catholic novelists. Both have remained in print continuously since their deaths. The Mexican episode is a chapter most accounts of either writer's career skip with a sentence or two.

{

• • •

}

Daniel sets the manuscript aside. The Greene-and-Waugh chapter has been the chapter of the pragmatic, politically entangled Catholic writers — the figures whose Catholicism was the cover under which they did, for a moment in 1938 and 1939, work for interests that the Catholic faith had no specific claim on.

What strikes Daniel about the pair, on rereading the chapter, is the way the great novels and the compromised journalism share the same author. *The Power and the Glory* is not less great because *The Lawless Roads* preceded it. *Brideshead Revisited* is not less great because *Robbery Under Law* preceded it. The serious Catholic literature of these two writers survives the political compromise of their late-1930s Mexican episode. The political compromise also remains, however, on the record. The two are not finally separable.

Daniel's view of the matter is, he acknowledges, particular. He is Mexican by birth and American by long choice — naturalized in 1979, after most of his working life had been spent in Washington and New York, proud of his US citizenship in the way that the choosing of a country can never quite be dislodged in a person who took the oath as an adult. But the Mexican identity has not been dissolved by the American one. The country these two writers traveled to in 1938 to denounce was the country he was born in nine years later.

The Cárdenas regime that they treated as a corrupt anti-Catholic socialist failure was the regime that had nationalized the oil that had been bleeding Mexican wealth into British and American shareholder accounts for two generations. The recurring charge in the propaganda — that Cárdenas was, in his sympathies and his trajectory, a communist — was inaccurate even as the propaganda was being written. Cárdenas had preserved private property; he had not advanced any Marxist ideology in his speeches or in his policies; he was, in his political identification, a Mexican revolutionary nationalist, not a member of the Comintern's project. He had remained close to the United States;

he had welcomed thousands of Spanish Republican refugees fleeing the Franco victory in 1939, opening a major immigration to Mexico that produced the Spanish-Republican-refounded schools Daniel had attended as a child; he would, three years after the publication of the Greene and Waugh books, declare war on Germany and Japan and align Mexico with the Allies in the Second World War. The country had begun, under his administration, the long slow climb out of the chronic political instability the post-revolutionary decades had imposed. Cárdenas had been, on the actual evidence, one of the better Mexican presidents of the twentieth century. The international propaganda campaign against him had been, on the actual evidence, what international propaganda campaigns funded by displaced foreign owners almost always are. Greene and Waugh had been, in this case, two of the more eloquent contributors to that campaign.

The copy of *Robbery Under Law* on the low shelf is the documentary remainder of the episode — the sponsored pamphlet that Waugh later disavowed without quite removing from the public record. Daniel keeps it for the same reason a constitutional lawyer keeps the briefs of cases he disagreed with — as evidence, as reminder, as the small private record of the difference between what the conventional reception of a writer celebrates and what the writer was actually willing to write when the commission came from the right quarter.

What the chapter has not done — and what Daniel has been deliberately holding off — is the question of whether a Catholicism this politically entangled is still, in any meaningful sense, the Catholicism that brought Pascal to fire and Newman to Littlemore and Stein to Auschwitz. The question is, Daniel thinks, the question the chapter cannot finally answer. Greene and Waugh were Catholics. Their Catholicism produced great novels and a compromised journalism. Both came out of the same religious commitment. The commitment was real. The compromise was also real. The book Daniel is writing makes room for both.

He closes the notebook. He goes to the listening chair. He chooses, this evening, William Byrd's *Mass for Five Voices* — the great work of English Catholic polyphony composed in secret during the 1590s, when the celebration of the Catholic Mass in England was a capital offense. Byrd was the great English Catholic composer of the recusant period; the Mass was sung clandestinely in private chapels of the recusant gentry. The recording is The Tallis Scholars under Peter Phillips. The *Kyrie* begins. The voices are restrained, as they must be in music written to be sung in a country where its singing could cost the life of the singer. Greene and Waugh had inherited, four centuries later, the small embattled English Catholic minority whose music this had been. They had been canonical members of that minority. They had also, at one moment, sold the minority's specific witness to interests that did not care about the minority.

Figures at the Threshold

Messiaen

Daniel sits at the desk. The Messiaen materials are out: the *Traité de rythme, de couleur, et d'ornithologie* in seven volumes; the conversations with Claude Samuel (*Music and Color*); the score of *Quatuor pour la fin du temps* in the Durand edition; the Hill and Simeone biography; Rebecca Rischin's *For the End of Time: The Story of the Messiaen Quartet*; recordings of the *Quatuor*, the *Vingt regards sur l'enfant Jésus*, *Saint François d'Assise* on the small shelf next to the listening chair.

Messiaen is the chapter the framework marked, from the beginning, as not quite a conversion. He was a lifelong Catholic. He was born a Catholic in 1908 in Avignon to devout Catholic parents, was raised in the practice, took the practice as the air he breathed his whole life, and never crossed any threshold of religious commitment because he had always been on the same side of every threshold. He is the only figure in the book whose Catholic faith was the inheritance rather than the chosen position.

The chapter earns its place, however, because the deepening of his Catholic faith produced one of the great religious works of the twentieth century under conditions that no other figure in the book had to confront. Captured by the Germans during the fall of France in June 1940, transported to a prisoner-of-war camp in Silesia, held for nine months at Stalag VIII-A in Görlitz on the German-Polish border, Messiaen composed and assembled a small ensemble for the *Quatuor pour la fin du temps — Quartet for the End of Time* — and conducted its first performance, in barrack 27 of the camp, on the freezing evening of January 15, 1941, before an audience of approximately four hundred prisoners and guards. The piece is one of the most concentrated artistic responses to extremity in the twentieth-century repertoire. It is also one of the most rigorous statements of Catholic mystical theology that any twentieth-century composer made in any musical form.

The chapter is the chapter of the deepening, not the conversion. The faith that did not have to be acquired produced, under the pressure of the camp and the war and the threatened end of European civilization, the work that articulated the faith with a clarity Messiaen had not been able to reach in the years of ordinary peace.

He writes the date at the top of the page: *15 January 1941.*

{

• • •

}

He had been born on December 10, 1908, in Avignon, into a household where the major formations of his life were already present in his parents. His father Pierre Messiaen was a literary scholar, the future translator of all of Shakespeare into French; his mother Cécile Sauvage was a poet of the symbolist generation, whose collection *L'Âme en bourgeon — The Soul in Bud —*

was written during her pregnancy with Olivier and was, in some sense she had foreseen, written *to* him. He grew up reading. He grew up musical. He grew up in a French Catholicism that was the natural medium of the household — the Mass, the saints' days, the integration of religious feeling into ordinary cultivated life. He never had to find his Catholicism. It was simply there.

He entered the Paris Conservatoire in 1919 at the age of eleven. He studied with Marcel Dupré in organ, with Paul Dukas in composition, with Maurice Emmanuel in musical history. He won the major composition prizes. In 1931, at twenty-two, he was appointed titular organist of La Trinité — the great Paris parish church on the boulevard Haussmann — a position he would hold, with the single interruption of his nine months as a German prisoner of war from June 1940 to March 1941, until his death in 1992. He would play for the parish Masses every Sunday for six decades, with that one absence in 1940 and 1941.

He married Claire Delbos, a violinist, in 1932; their son Pascal was born in 1937. He founded the group La Jeune France in 1936 with André Jolivet, Daniel-Lesur, and Yves Baudrier — a small association of young French composers proposing a return to spiritual seriousness against the neoclassicism that had dominated French composition in the 1920s. The major works of the 1930s — *La Nativité du Seigneur*, the great organ cycle of nine meditations on the Nativity composed in 1935; *Les Corps glorieux*, the seven meditations on the resurrected body composed in 1939 — established him as the leading figure of his generation in Catholic sacred music.

{

• • •

}

He had been drafted into the French Army in September 1939, at the outbreak of the war. His vision was poor; he was assigned as a medical auxiliary rather than as a combatant.

The German invasion of France began on May 10, 1940. The French defensive line collapsed in three weeks. By the end of May the British had been pushed off the continent at Dunkirk; by mid-June the German army was in Paris. The French army surrendered. Messiaen was captured in early June 1940, near Verdun. He was thirty-one. He was transported, with tens of thousands of other French prisoners, to Stalag VIII-A in Görlitz — a town on the Neisse River in Lower Silesia, on what is now the border between Germany and Poland. The camp held perhaps thirty thousand prisoners. Conditions were the conditions of the Wehrmacht's prisoner-of-war camps in the early period of the war: cramped barracks, inadequate rations, extreme cold in winter, work details, the small daily indignities.

In the first weeks at Stalag VIII-A, Messiaen identified three other musicians among the prisoners. Étienne Pasquier was a cellist, formerly of the celebrated Pasquier Trio in Paris. Henri Akoka was a clarinettist, an Algerian-born French Jew, a member of the Orchestre National. Jean Le Boulaire was a violinist, a younger man, a recent Conservatoire graduate. The four of them found each other within the first month.

The camp had a German officer who took an interest in the prisoners' cultural life. *Hauptmann* Carl-Albert Brüll was a Silesian lawyer in civilian life, a man whose attitude toward his prisoners would become, in the eyes of those who knew him, one of the small and surprising acts of decency that the German army of 1940-41 occasionally produced. Brüll arranged for instruments to be brought into the camp. The cello had a missing string. The piano had several keys that did not work. The violin and the clarinet were in tolerable condition. Brüll found Messiaen a small room off one of the barracks where he could compose; he provided paper, pencils, and the basic supplies the work required.

Messiaen had brought one book with him into captivity. The book was a small French Bible. He had, before his capture, been reading the Apocalypse of Saint John — the Book of Revelation — in connection with a planned set of meditations he had not yet composed. The Apocalypse had been on his mind when the army was captured. The Apocalypse was on his mind in the camp.

The decision to compose a chamber work for the four available musicians was made in the late summer of 1940. The work would be eight movements long — eight in the medieval Christian symbolism for eternity, the day of the resurrection that follows the seven days of creation. The work would be called *Quatuor pour la fin du temps — Quartet for the End of Time.* The title was from chapter ten of Revelation: an angel comes down from heaven, sets one foot on the sea and one on the land, lifts his hand, and swears by the eternal that *time shall be no more.*

{

• • •

}

He composed across the autumn of 1940 and into the early winter. The cold in the camp was severe; the unheated barrack room where he worked was, in November and December, below freezing for most of the day. He wore his French army overcoat as he composed. The ink froze in the inkwell at night.

The work that emerged is one of the most theologically and musically rigorous chamber pieces of the twentieth century. Eight movements, each engaging a specific theological theme and a specific musical innovation Messiaen had been developing in the previous decade.

The opening movement — *Liturgie de cristal* — is a *crystal liturgy*: the awakening of the birds at dawn before the angel arrives. The clarinet has the song of the blackbird; the violin has the song of the nightingale; the cello and piano provide the harmonic ground. The musical materials are Messiaen's *modes of limited transposition*, the symmetric scales he had been working with since the late 1920s, and his characteristic *non-retrogradable rhythms* — rhythmic figures that read identically forward and backward, mirror-symmetric in time, evoking eternity by the suspension of temporal directionality.

The third movement, *Abîme des oiseaux* — *Abyss of Birds* — is for solo clarinet, the abyss being time itself with its weariness, the birds being the opposite, the ascent toward joy.

The fifth and eighth movements are the great *louanges* — *Praises*. *Louange à l'Éternité de Jésus*, for cello and piano, is a slow extended cantilena over a piano harmonic ground; *Louange à l'Immortalité de Jésus*, for violin and piano, mirrors it in the closing position of the work. The two movements together — the fifth a praise of the Eternity of Jesus, the eighth a praise of the Immortality of Jesus — are, on Messiaen's own testimony, the theological center of the work. They use the slowest tempo Messiaen ever wrote, indicated as *infiniment lent, extatique* — infinitely slow, ecstatic. The cello in the fifth and the violin in the eighth move at almost the speed of breath; the piano provides a quiet harmonic descent. The two movements are among the most concentrated meditations on eternity that Western music has produced.

The fourth and sixth movements — *Intermède* and *Danse de la fureur, pour les sept trompettes* — are the more violent material: the *Dance of Fury for the Seven Trumpets* is for all four players in unison, in Messiaen's most aggressive rhythmic language, evoking the seven angels with the seven trumpets of the Apocalypse who bring the catastrophes that precede the end of time.

The work refuses, by design, to develop in the standard Western symphonic manner. It progresses, instead, by the juxtaposition of contemplative tableaux and apocalyptic fury. It ends in eternity, with the violin's slow ascent to a high E held in the *infiniment lent* of the closing measure, into a silence the piece does not, finally, break.

{

• • •

}

The performance was scheduled for the evening of January 15, 1941. The temperature in the camp was below freezing. The sky was overcast. The barrack chosen was barrack 27, one of the larger barracks of the camp, which on this evening was packed with approximately four hundred listeners — French and Polish prisoners in the main, with German guards along the walls, and *Hauptmann* Brüll and several other German officers in the front rows. The audience included men of every educational and social background, most of whom had not, in any prior period of their lives, attended a concert of contemporary chamber music.

The four musicians took their places. Pasquier had a cello with three strings — the lowest string was missing — and had rewritten the cello part to accommodate the absence. Akoka had a clarinet that, in the cold, was difficult to play in tune. Le Boulaire had a violin that had been borrowed from a French priest among the prisoners. Messiaen had a piano with several keys that did not work, around which he had revised the piano part.

The performance began. The opening of *Liturgie de cristal* — the dawn awakening of the birds, the clarinet's blackbird and the violin's nightingale — entered the cold barrack and was, for the four hundred men listening, the first sound of contemporary art most of them had heard since their mobilization. The work moved through its eight movements over the course of approximately fifty minutes. The audience did not applaud between movements; they were listening with the attention of men for whom the music was new and the situation extreme.

When the final movement ended — the violin's slow ascent into the *infiniment lent* of the closing measure, the piano's quiet harmonic descent into silence — the silence held in the barrack for some seconds before the applause began.

Messiaen later said it had been, of all the performances of his work in his sixty-year career, the one in which he had felt most certainly understood. The audience had been, he said, the most attentive he had ever played for. The conditions had been the worst he had ever performed under. The work had landed.

Akoka, the clarinettist — who as a Jew was in particular danger in the camp — said in interviews many years later that the *Quartet* was the moment in his captivity that had given him the courage to believe he might survive. He did survive; he escaped from a prisoner train in 1941 and made his way back to North Africa. The other three were released later in 1941, on forged or expedited papers that Brüll arranged.

{

• • •

}

Messiaen was released from Stalag VIII-A in March 1941 and returned to Paris and to La Trinité, which he would now hold for another fifty-one years.

The fifty years that followed produced what is, by general agreement, the most significant body of religious-musical work composed in the twentieth century. *Visions de l'Amen* (1943) for two pianos. *Vingt regards sur l'enfant Jésus* (1944) — the great cycle for solo piano on the Nativity, twenty meditations from the silence of the contemplating Father to the hand-clapping of the Magi. The *Turangalîla-Symphonie* (1948) for orchestra, ten movements on the Tristan and Iseult myth, commissioned by Koussevitzky. The *Catalogue d'oiseaux* (1956-58) for piano, the great encyclopedic engagement with French birdsong. *Et exspecto resurrectionem mortuorum* (1964), commissioned by André Malraux for a public commemoration of the dead of the World Wars at Sainte-Chapelle. *La Transfiguration de Notre Seigneur Jésus-Christ* (1965-69), the seventy-minute oratorio. *Saint François d'Assise* (1975-83), the great late opera, premiered at the Paris Opéra in 1983.

He taught harmony and analysis at the Conservatoire from 1942; from 1966, the chair of composition. His students included Boulez, Stockhausen, Xenakis, George Benjamin.

His first wife Claire Delbos suffered from severe progressive mental illness in the 1950s and was institutionalized; she died in 1959. Messiaen married Yvonne Loriod, his pupil and the major interpreter of his piano music, in 1961.

He died in Paris on April 27, 1992, at eighty-three. He was buried in the cemetery of Saint-Théoffrey in Isère, near Petichet. The grave is simple. The inscription includes the words from Revelation: *Et tempus non erit amplius.* And there shall be time no more.

{

• • •

}

Daniel sets the manuscript aside. The Messiaen chapter has been the chapter of the deepening rather than the conversion — the figure whose Catholic faith was the inheritance and not the discovery, who never had to cross a threshold because he had always been on the inside, but whose deepening of the inheritance under the conditions of the prisoner-of-war camp produced one of the great religious works of the twentieth century.

What strikes Daniel about Messiaen is the relationship between the form of the *Quartet* and the conditions of its composition. The *Quartet* is not a piece of music *about* the camp. It does not contain references to the camp. It does not protest, in any direct way, against the German army or the war or the catastrophes of European civilization in the 1940s. It is, instead, a meditation on the eternity of Christ and the immortality of Christ. The eternity is what the camp could not touch. The immortality is what no political or military catastrophe could remove. The work refuses, by its very structure — the *non-retrogradable rhythms*, the *modes of limited transposition*, the *infiniment lent* of the *louanges* — to be inside historical time at all. It is set against time. The angel of the eighth chapter of the Apocalypse who lifts his hand and swears that *time shall be no more* is, in Messiaen's reading, the figure who frees the work from the conditions of its composition.

This is, Daniel thinks, the most rigorous case the book contains of the relationship between art and religious commitment. The work is great precisely because the religious commitment is not a decoration. It is the structure. The eight movements are, on Messiaen's own theological reading, the medieval Christian eight — the seven days of creation plus the eighth day of resurrection. The two great *louanges* are, in their slowness, the musical embodiment of the doctrine they articulate. The *non-retrogradable rhythms* are the musical embodiment of the theological claim that eternity is not a long time but the absence of time as a directional substance.

For Daniel — the secular reader who has been listening to Messiaen with attention and admiration for fifty years — the chapter raises a question the book has not previously raised quite this sharply. Is the work intelligible to him in the way the *Quartet*'s Catholic theological framework would require? Or is he listening to it as one listens to any great work of art, with the structure of meaning provided by the work and the religious commitment of the listener not required for the structure to do its work?

Daniel's honest answer is that he listens to Messiaen the way he listens to Bach — with full attention to the musical and structural integrity, with full respect for the theological framework that produced the music, and without himself sharing the theological commitment. The work survives the listener's secular position. The work also reminds the secular listener that there are kinds of work that the secular position alone could not have produced.

He closes the notebook. He goes to the listening chair. He chooses, this evening, the *Quatuor pour la fin du temps* in the recording by the Tashi ensemble — Peter Serkin on piano, Ida

Kavafian on violin, Fred Sherry on cello, Richard Stoltzman on clarinet — recorded in 1975 for Deutsche Grammophon, the standard recording of his generation. The opening of *Liturgie de cristal* begins. The clarinet's blackbird at dawn enters first. The violin's nightingale answers. The cold barrack at Görlitz, eighty-five years ago, fills the apartment.

Figures at the Threshold

Pärt

Daniel sits at the desk. The Pärt materials are out: the *Lamentate* and *Tabula Rasa* scores in the Universal Edition; the Paul Hillier monograph *Arvo Pärt*; the Geoff Smith collected interviews; Peter Bouteneff's *Arvo Pärt: Out of Silence*; a small selection of essays by Pärt himself. On the small shelf next to the listening chair, the recordings: *Tabula Rasa* in the Manfred Eicher / ECM 1984 recording — the album that introduced Pärt to the West and remains one of the most influential classical recordings of the late twentieth century — and the various subsequent ECM releases that have continued for forty years now, with Hillier and his ensembles, with Tõnu Kaljuste, with the Hilliard Ensemble.

Pärt is the book's closing figure. He is the second musician of the twentieth century in the collection, after Schoenberg and Messiaen, but he occupies a position different from either. Schoenberg's musical revolution had preceded his return to Judaism and continued after it; the music and the religious return were two arcs in the same life that ran on parallel rather than congruent tracks. Messiaen's Catholicism had been the inheritance, the constant; the music came out of the constant rather than producing the religious commitment. Pärt is the figure for whom the conversion to Russian Orthodoxy, the years of compositional silence, and the emergence of a wholly new musical language — *tintinnabuli* — are not three things but one thing, occurring across the same interval of his life and producing each other. The conversion is the music. The music is the conversion. There is no other case in the book where the religious turning and the artistic method are this intimate.

The chapter is the chapter of the conversion-into-method. It compresses around the years 1968 to 1977 — the period in Soviet Estonia in which Pärt withdrew from composition, immersed himself in early sacred music and Orthodox liturgy, was received into the Russian Orthodox Church, and emerged with the new method. The decisive moment, if there is a single decisive moment, is the composition of *Für Alina* in 1976 — the small two-minute piano piece that is the founding work of *tintinnabuli*, the moment the religious-musical synthesis first found its formal expression.

He writes the date at the top of the page: *Tallinn, 1976.*

{

• • •

}

He had been born in Paide, Estonia, on September 11, 1935. Estonia had been independent for fifteen years at the time of his birth, having achieved independence from the Russian Empire in 1920. The family was Lutheran by background — Estonian Lutheranism being the standard religious form of the country — though only nominally observant. The independence ended in 1940 when the Soviet Union annexed Estonia under the Hitler-Stalin Pact; Pärt was four. He grew up under Soviet rule.

He showed musical talent early. He entered the Tallinn Conservatory in 1957 to study composition with Heino Eller, who had been the major Estonian composition teacher of the previous generation. Pärt was twenty-two when he started; he had already done his obligatory Soviet military service and had worked as a recording engineer at Estonian Radio.

The Soviet musical environment of the late 1950s and early 1960s was a particular one. The Khrushchev Thaw had relaxed the Stalinist orthodoxy on socialist realism. Composers in the Soviet republics — particularly in the Baltic republics, which had a more European-facing intellectual culture than the Russian heartland — had begun to experiment with the modernist techniques that had been developed in the West. The experimentation was monitored by the Composers' Union and was permitted within limits. Pärt was one of the most talented of his generation in this experimentation. His First Symphony of 1963 was a serial work that drew specifically on Schoenberg, Webern, and the Polish school. His *Perpetuum Mobile* of 1963 was a tightly-woven serial piece. Through the mid-1960s he wrote a series of works in this avant-garde register.

He was also, throughout this period, the principal composer of music for Estonian radio and film. The Soviet system supported him through these commissions; he wrote scores for over fifty films. The work paid the bills; it also kept him within the system's expectations.

{

• • •

}

By 1968 Pärt had begun to feel that the avant-garde register was no longer adequate to what he wanted music to do. The crisis, when he spoke about it later, had several layers. The Soviet political environment was tightening — the Brezhnev years had begun, the Prague Spring had been crushed by Warsaw Pact tanks in August 1968, the brief opening of the Khrushchev period was over. The avant-garde, for Pärt, had also been a position dependent on the dialogue with Western modernism — and the dialogue, as the political tightening proceeded, became increasingly impossible to maintain. The Western modernist project had its own internal crisis; the Soviet system was tightening. Pärt was, in 1968, thirty-three years old, with a major early body of work, and at a loss as to what to write next.

He composed almost nothing for the next eight years.

The silence was deliberate. He did not stop being a composer. He stopped composing in the public sense. He had, with his second wife Nora — whom he had met in the mid-1960s and married in 1972 — withdrawn into a period of intensive listening and study. The materials he listened to and studied were almost entirely from the early Christian sacred-music tradition: Gregorian chant, in the recordings that had begun to circulate in the West and that were available in tapes that crossed the Soviet border slowly; the polyphonic school of Notre-Dame de Paris from the twelfth and thirteenth centuries — Léonin, Pérotin, the early organum; the Ars Nova of Machaut; the Renaissance polyphony of Josquin and Palestrina; the Russian Orthodox liturgical chant tradition that he could hear in the small Russian Orthodox churches that operated, with limited tolerance from the Soviet authorities, in Tallinn.

What he was doing in those years, he later said, was unlearning. The avant-garde training had taught him a particular way of organizing musical material. The early Christian polyphony had organized material differently — by counterpoint of independent voices over modal centers, by long-breath unaccompanied lines, by the interplay of chant and the floating organum. The material had a different grammar. He needed to learn that grammar before he could write anything new.

He was also, during this period, increasingly serious about Russian Orthodox practice. He and Nora attended liturgies; they consulted with the local Orthodox priest; they were received into the Russian Orthodox Church at some point in the early 1970s — the date is not perfectly documented, but the most reliable accounts place the formal reception around 1972. They became members of the small Russian-speaking Orthodox community in Tallinn.

The conversion was not, in any documented account, dramatic. It was the public form catching up with what had become, across several years of liturgy and study, the interior settlement.

{

• • •

}

The new method emerged in 1976. The first work in it was a small two-minute piano piece called *Für Alina* — *For Alina* — written for the daughter of a friend who was studying piano. The piece is two staves of music. The right hand plays a slow stepwise melodic line in B minor — what Pärt would call the M-voice, the *melody-voice* — moving up and down the natural minor scale with no chromatic inflection. The left hand plays a series of three-note chords drawn from the B-minor triad — the T-voice, the *tintinnabuli-voice*, the bell-tone voice that simply rings the home triad in different octave and inversion arrangements.

The two voices move together. They do not modulate. They do not develop in any conventional sense. They simply unfold, with the M-voice's stepwise motion against the T-voice's triadic ringing, for two minutes, until the piece ends. The total musical material is very small. The musical effect is almost overwhelming — a stillness, a luminosity, a sense of suspension in time that the music produces by what it refuses to do.

Tintinnabuli — from the Latin for *little bell* — was the name Pärt gave to the method. The bell was the central image. He had been listening to bells for years, in the Orthodox church towers of Tallinn, in the recordings of the Russian liturgical bell-ringing tradition. The bell, when struck, produces a fundamental pitch and a complex set of overtones that give the bell-sound its characteristic ring. *Tintinnabuli* music was, in Pärt's understanding, the music that organized itself around the bell-tone — the home triad ringing as the T-voice, the melodic line moving stepwise around it as the M-voice. The two voices were, in his theological reading, an image: the M-voice was the human soul moving in time; the T-voice was the divine ground that did not move and to which the soul was always related.

Für Alina was followed quickly by the major early *tintinnabuli* works. *Cantus in Memoriam Benjamin Britten* — for string orchestra and bell — was completed in 1977, in response to Britten's death the previous year. *Tabula Rasa* — for two solo violins, prepared piano, and string orchestra, in two movements — was completed in 1977 and premiered in Tallinn in September of that year. *Fratres*, the work that exists in many subsequent versions for different instruments, was first composed in 1977. *Summa*, the choral setting of the Credo, came in the same year. *Spiegel im Spiegel* — *Mirror in Mirror* — for violin and piano, came in 1978.

These are now among the most-performed works of any twentieth-century composer. They were composed, in 1976-1978, in a small Soviet republic by a man who had emerged from eight years of silence with a method that had no precise precedent in twentieth-century music and that would, within a decade, redefine what was possible in classical sacred music.

{

• • •

}

The Soviet authorities had not been comfortable with Pärt's religious turn. The avant-garde music had been within the system's tolerated range; the Orthodox conversion and the subsequent sacred works moved him into a more difficult position. By the late 1970s the pressure had increased. Nora's Jewish background added a further layer of political vulnerability. In January 1980 Pärt and Nora and their two sons applied for and received permission to emigrate. They left Tallinn, traveled to Vienna, and were received by the Austrian musical community, which gave Pärt temporary citizenship and resources.

In 1981 the family moved to West Berlin, where the German Academic Exchange Service had arranged a year-long residency. They stayed. Berlin became home for the next thirty years.

The Berlin years produced the major works of Pärt's mature career. *Passio Domini Nostri Iesu Christi secundum Joannem — The Passion of Our Lord Jesus Christ According to John* — was completed in 1982. *Stabat Mater* in 1985. *Te Deum* in 1985. *Miserere* in 1989. *Berliner Messe* in 1990. *Litany* in 1994. The works grew larger; the international performances accelerated; ECM Records under Manfred Eicher had begun, in 1984, with the *Tabula Rasa* album, to present Pärt to a Western audience that had not previously known he existed.

By the early 2000s Pärt was, by some measures, the most-performed living classical composer in the world. He returned to Estonia in 2010, after thirty years in Berlin; he settled in Laulasmaa, on the coast about forty kilometers west of Tallinn. The Arvo Pärt Centre opened there in 2018 — a building designed by the Spanish architects Nieto Sobejano, with a small chapel, archive, and library. He is, at the time Daniel writes this chapter, ninety years old. He has continued to compose into his late eighties — *Adam's Lament* in 2009, the small later works that have continued to appear.

{

• • •

}

Daniel sets the manuscript aside. The Pärt chapter has been the chapter of the conversion-into-method — the figure for whom the religious turning and the musical revolution were the same event, occurring across the same eight years in Soviet Estonia between 1968 and 1976, and producing in their convergence one of the major bodies of late-twentieth-century sacred music.

What strikes Daniel about Pärt, on rereading the chapter, is the exactness of the parallel between the religious commitment and the formal method. *Tintinnabuli* is, in its musical structure, an articulation of an Orthodox theological position. The T-voice, the bell-tone of the home triad, is the unmoved, the divine ground; the M-voice, the stepwise melody, is the soul moving in time around the ground; the two are inseparable; the moving voice is always related to the unmoving one; the unmoving one is always present beneath the moving one. The Orthodox understanding of the relation of the soul to God — the *theosis* of the Eastern tradition, the gradual deification by participation in the divine energies — is the theological structure. The musical structure embodies it. The two are, on Pärt's testimony and in the actual hearing of the music, the same structure.

This is, Daniel thinks, the closing case of the book. He has watched, across fifteen chapters, the various ways the religious commitment can produce its formal expression — the mystical experience that produces the *Pensées*, the philosophical conversion that produces the *Apologia*, the slow scholarly absorption that produces the *Heart Sutra* translations, the second-generation inheritance that produces the *Matthäuspassion* revival, the camp deepening that produces the *Quartet for the End of Time*. Pärt is the case in which the production is direct: the religious turning *is* the musical method; there is no gap between the conversion and the form.

For Daniel — who has not, on his own evidence, been called — the chapter raises the closing question of the book. What is it that the figures the book has been studying have access to, that he has not? He has read what they read. He has listened to what they listened to. He has visited the buildings they prayed in. He has sat through the offices, on tourist terms, that they sat through as participants. He has not, at any point in his sixty years of patient secular attention, been moved to cross the threshold the figures have crossed. The book does not answer the question. The book has been, all along, the form in which the question can be asked carefully, by a witness who refuses to pretend that the question is settled.

He closes the notebook. He goes to the listening chair. He

chooses, this evening, Pärt's *Cantus in Memoriam Benjamin Britten* — the six-minute work for string orchestra and bell composed in 1977, the year of *Tabula Rasa* and *Fratres* and *Summa,* the year the new method announced itself to the world. The recording is the Manfred Eicher ECM with the Lithuanian Chamber Orchestra. The bell sounds. The strings descend in slow canonic lines that fold inward toward an A-minor cadence. The piece ends. The bell continues, fades, ends.

A Note on the Collaboration

This book was written in active partnership with Claude, an artificial intelligence developed by Anthropic. The collaboration began with a question — a conversation with a friend about religious conversion in old age, and an exposure to David Runciman's podcast series on political conversions — that the author wished to pursue at the scale of a literary inquiry rather than an essay. What emerged across the months of writing was something closer to a sustained writing dialogue than a tool-and-user transaction.

The ideas, the philosophical architecture, the choice of figures, and the creative decisions at every level originated with the author. A partial record of his specific contributions gives a clearer picture of how the work was shaped:

- Conceiving the project as a sequence of historical-fiction novellas about religious conversion, framed by a contemporary narrator, rather than as essays or a conventional study
- Choosing the title *Figures at the Threshold*
- Establishing Daniel Ferrara as the frame narrator — Mexican-born, of Spanish-Sephardic origin through Puglia and Mexico, Yale-trained, married to a New Orleans Catholic, naturalized American in 1979, retired constitu-

tional lawyer, widower of three years, agnostic — and Beacon Court on East 58th Street as the apartment from which the inquiry is conducted

- Selecting and revising the figure list across the long process of composition: adding Heine, Felix Mendelssohn (as the second-generation portrait), Greene and Waugh, Pärt, Messiaen, and Walter Benjamin alongside Simone Weil; selecting Edward Conze rather than Blavatsky/Olcott as the Buddhist case; setting the eventual list at fifteen historical figures
- Setting the chapter scale: from the original novella scale of fifteen to twenty-five thousand words down to the final long-short-story scale of twenty-five hundred to three thousand words per chapter
- Specifying the form: third-person close on the historical figure for the bodies of the chapters; first-person stream-of-consciousness in Daniel's voice for the prologue and the frame openings and closes; the formal correspondence with the author's previous novel *Trying to Understand What is Happening*
- Contributing the Sutton Towers anecdote in the Pascal chapter — the apartment in Washington with the twelve-foot window facing the National Cathedral, the joke about waiting for a signal that Marie-Claire did not appreciate
- Contributing the La Tourette anecdote in the Huysmans chapter — the night sixty years ago at the Le Corbusier-designed Dominican convent near Lyon, the cell with the small terrace, the cold autumn night under the stars, the Jewish friend, the Mass next morning
- Contributing the woman on the floor in the Stein chapter — the four apartments per floor at Beacon Court, the woman

in her early forties whose loneliness has saddened him for some time, the chapter's recognition of his own habit of empathy

- Specifying the empathy theme as the moral center of Daniel's private life, and connecting it to Stein's 1916 dissertation *Zum Problem der Einfühlung*
- Specifying the death-and-health reflection in the Rosenzweig chapter — Daniel at seventy-eight set against Rosenzweig at thirty-five, the absence of an Edith
- Adding Schopenhauer and Hesse as German precursors and fellow-travelers in the Conze chapter, and the four affinities between philosophical Buddhism and liberal-individualist principles (personal responsibility, self-reliance, respect for pluralism, the line drawn at extremism)
- Insisting on historical accuracy in the Greene and Waugh chapter on the Mexican Church-State context — the 1857 Constitution and the comparison with the French model, the Vatican's role in the 1926 closing of the churches, the limited geography of the Cristero War, Cárdenas as a revolutionary nationalist rather than a communist, Cárdenas's reception of the Spanish Republican refugees and his Allied alignment in WWII
- Specifying the *sponsored pamphlet* framing for Waugh's *Robbery Under Law*, with Daniel's second-hand copy on the low shelf as the documentary anchor
- Adding the Mann / *Doktor Faustus* episode to the Schoenberg chapter, and the larger émigré context of Germany's intellectual loss
- Choosing the closing music for many of the chapters — the Bach *Magnificat* for Claudel, Bruch's *Kol Nidrei* for Rosen-

zweig, the Du Pré recording specifically; Schoenberg's *Kol Nidre* op. 39 for Schoenberg himself; the Solesmes chant for Weil; the Tashi recording for Messiaen; the Cantus for Pärt

- Specifying the Rimbaud passage in the Claudel chapter — the *Lettre du Voyant* of 1871, the anti-clerical poems, the persistent preoccupation with God beneath the blasphemy
- Setting the title and subtitle in their final form — *Figures at the Threshold: A Novel in Fifteen Religious Conversions*

Claude's role was to give those contributions literary form — drafting chapters, developing the third-person close prose of the historical novellas, finding the precise sentence that carried the weight of a complex thought, sustaining the philosophical and tonal coherence of the text across the prologue and sixteen chapters, and returning faithfully to the corrections and clarifications that the author asked for in each pass.

The result is a book that is entirely the author's — in conception, in judgment, in voice — and honestly collaborative in its making. That distinction matters, and it is the reason the collaboration is named here rather than hidden in a footnote.

www.ingramcontent.com/pod-product-compliance
Lightning Source LLC
LaVergne TN
LVHW100527110826
845146LV00002B/803